A CREED COUNTRY *Christmas*

Also available from
LINDA LAEL MILLER

The Montana Creeds
LOGAN
DYLAN
TYLER

The McKettricks
McKETTRICK'S CHOICE
McKETTRICK'S LUCK
McKETTRICK'S PRIDE
McKETTRICK'S HEART
A McKETTRICK CHRISTMAS

The Mojo Sheepshanks series
DEADLY GAMBLE
DEADLY DECEPTIONS

The Stone Creek series
THE MAN FROM STONE CREEK
A WANTED MAN
THE RUSTLER
THE BRIDEGROOM

McKettricks of Texas
TATE
GARRETT
AUSTIN

LINDA LAEL MILLER

A CREED COUNTRY *Christmas*

HARLEQUIN® MIRA®

Published in Great Britain 2013.
Harlequin MIRA, an imprint of Harlequin (UK) Limited,
Eton House, 18-24 Paradise Road,
Richmond, Surrey, TW9 1SR

ISBN 978 1 848 45269 5

63-1113

Harlequin's policy is to use papers that are natural, renewable and recyclable products and made from wood grown in sustainable forests. The logging and manufacturing processes conform to the legal environmental regulations of the country of origin.

Printed and bound in Spain
by Blackprint CPI, Barcelona

Dear Reader,

When those hell-raising Creed brothers—Logan, Dylan and Tyler—came home to Big Sky Country to put down roots, the former rodeo cowboys created quite a ruckus with the women. Which raised the question for me and all you readers out there: where did those rascals learn their rowdy, romancing ways? Relax, my friends, while I take you back to 1910 and Stillwater Springs for a holiday visit with the man behind the legends: Lincoln Creed. This cowboy with a Montana-size heart aims to lasso strong-willed Juliana Mitchell, a woman with a mission and a serious attitude.

I also wanted to write today to tell you about a special group of people with whom I've recently become involved. It is The Humane Society of the United States (HSUS), specifically their Pets for Life programme.

The Pets for Life programme is one of the best ways to help your local shelter: that is, to help keep animals out of shelters in the first place. Something as basic as keeping a collar and tag on your pet all the time, so if he gets out and gets lost, he can be returned home. Being a responsible pet owner. Spaying or neutering your pet. And not giving up when things don't go perfectly. If your dog digs in the yard, or your cat scratches the furniture, know that these are problems that can be addressed. You can find all the information about these—and many other—common problems at www.petsforlife.org. This campaign is focused on keeping pets and their people together for a lifetime.

As many of you know, my own household includes two dogs, two cats and four horses, so this is a cause that is near and dear to my heart. I hope you'll get involved along with me.

May you be blessed.

With love,

For Jean Woofter
With love and gratitude

Chapter One

Stillwater Springs, Montana
December 20, 1910

The interior of Willand's Mercantile, redolent of saddle leather and wood smoke, seemed to recede as Juliana Mitchell stood at the counter, holding her breath.

The letter had *finally* arrived.

The letter Juliana had waited for, prayed for, repeatedly inquired after—at considerable cost to her pride—and, paradoxically, dreaded.

Her heart hitched painfully as she accepted the envelope

from the storekeeper's outstretched hand; the handwriting, a slanted scrawl penned in black ink, was definitely her brother Clay's. The postmark read Denver.

In the distance, the snow-muffled shrill of a train whistle announced the imminent arrival of the four o'clock from Missoula, which passed through town only once a week, bound for points south.

Juliana was keenly aware of the four children still in her charge, waiting just inside the door of a place where they knew they were patently unwelcome. She turned away from the counter—and the storekeeper's disapproving gaze—to fumble with the circle of red wax bearing Clay's imposing seal.

Please, God, she prayed silently. *Please.*

After drawing a deep breath and releasing it slowly, Juliana bit her lower lip, took out the single sheet folded inside.

Her heart, heretofore wedged into her throat, plummeted to the soles of her practical shoes. Her vision blurred.

Her brother hadn't enclosed the desperately needed funds she'd asked for—money that was rightfully her own, a part of the legacy her grandmother had left her. She could not purchase train tickets for herself and her charges, and the Indian School, their home and hers for the past two years, was no longer government property. The small but sturdy building had been sold to a neighboring farmer, and he planned to stable cows inside it.

Now the plank floor seemed to buckle slightly under Juliana's feet. The heat from the potbellied stove in the center of the store, so welcome only a few minutes before when she and the children had come in out of the blustery cold, all of them dappled with fat flakes of snow, threatened to smother Juliana now.

The little bell over the door jingled, indicating the arrival of another customer, but Juliana did not look up from the page in her hand. The words swam before her, making no more sense to her fitful mind than ancient Hebrew would have done.

A brief, frenzied hope stirred within Juliana. Perhaps all was not lost, perhaps Clay, not trusting the postal service, had *wired* the money she needed. It might be waiting for her, at that very moment, just down the street at the telegraph office.

Her eyes stung with the swift and sobering realization that she was grasping at straws. She blinked and forced herself to read what her older brother and legal guardian had written.

My Dear Sister,

I trust this letter will find you well.

Nora, the children and I are all in robust health. Your niece and nephew constantly inquire as to your whereabouts, as do certain other parties.

I regret that I cannot in good conscience remit the funds you have requested, for reasons that should be obvious to you....

Juliana crumpled the sheet of expensive vellum, nearly ill with disappointment and the helpless frustration that generally resulted from any dealings with her brother, direct or indirect.

"Are you all right, miss?" a male voice asked, strong and quiet.

Startled, Juliana looked up, saw a tall man standing directly in front of her. His eyes and hair were dark, the round brim of his hat and the shoulders of his long coat dusted with snow.

Waiting politely for her answer, he took off his hat. Hung it from the post of a wooden chair, smiled.

"I'm Lincoln Creed," he said, gruffly kind, pulling off a leather glove before extending his hand.

Juliana hesitated, offered her own hand in return. She knew the name, of course—the Creeds owned the largest cattle ranch in that part of the state, and the *Stillwater Springs Courier,* too. Although Juliana had had encounters with Weston, the brother who ran the newspaper, and briefly met the Widow Creed, the matriarch of the family, she'd never crossed paths with Lincoln.

"Juliana Mitchell," she said, with the proper balance of reticence and politeness. She'd been gently raised, after all. A hundred years ago—*a thousand*—she'd called one of the finest mansions in Denver home. She'd worn imported silks and velvets and fashionable hats, ridden in carriages with liveried drivers and even footmen.

Remembering made her faintly ashamed.

All that, of course, had been before her fall from social grace.

Before Clay, as administrator of their grandmother's estate, had all but disinherited her.

Mr. Creed dropped his gaze to the letter. "Bad news?" he asked, with an unsettling note of discernment. He might have had Indian blood himself, with his high cheekbones and raven-black hair.

The train whistle gave another triumphant squeal. It

had pulled into the rickety little depot at the edge of town, right on schedule. Passengers would alight, others would board. Mail and freight would be loaded and unloaded. And then the engine would chug out of the station, the line of cars rattling behind it.

A full week would pass before another train came through.

In the meantime, Juliana and the children would have no choice but to throw themselves upon the uncertain mercies of the townspeople. In a larger community, she might have turned to a church for assistance, but there weren't any in Stillwater Springs. The faithful met sporadically, in the one-room schoolhouse where only white students were allowed when the circuit preacher came through.

Juliana swallowed, wanting to cry, and determined that she wouldn't. "I'm afraid it *is* bad news," she admitted in belated answer to Mr. Creed's question.

He took a gentle hold on her elbow, escorted her to one of the empty wooden chairs over by the potbellied stove. Sat her down. "Did somebody die?" he asked.

Numb with distraction, Juliana shook her head.

What in the world was she going to do now? Without money, she could not purchase train tickets for herself and the children, or even arrange for temporary lodgings of some sort.

Mr. Creed inclined his head toward the children lined up in front of the display window, with its spindly but glittering Christmas tree. They'd turned their backs now, to look at the decorations and the elaborate toys tucked into the branches and arranged attractively underneath.

"I guess you must be the teacher from out at the Indian School," he said.

Mr. Willand, the mercantile's proprietor, interrupted with a *harrumph* sound.

Juliana ached as she watched the children. The storekeeper was keeping a close eye on them, too. Like so many people, he reasoned that simply because they were Indians, they were sure to steal, afforded the slightest opportunity. "Yes," she replied, practiced at ignoring such attitudes, if not resigned to them. "Or, at least, I *was*. The school is closed now."

Lincoln Creed nodded after skewering Mr. Willand with a glare. "I was sorry to hear it," he told her.

"No letters came since you were in here last week, Lincoln," Willand broke in, with some satisfaction. The very atmosphere of that store, overheated and close, seemed to bristle with mutual dislike. "Reckon you can wait around and see if there were any on today's train, but my guess is you wasted your money, putting all those advertisements in all them newspapers."

"Everyone is sorry, Mr. Creed," Juliana said quietly. "But no one seems inclined to help."

Momentarily distracted by Mr. Willand's remark, Lincoln didn't respond immediately. When he did, his voice was nearly drowned out by the scream of the train whistle.

Juliana stood up, remembered anew that her situation was hopeless, and sat down again, hard, all the strength gone from her knees. Perhaps she'd used it up, walking the two miles into town from the school, with every one of her worldly possessions tucked into a single worn-out satchel. Each of the children had carried a small bundle, too, leaving them on the sidewalk outside the door of the mercantile with Juliana's bag.

"There's a storm coming, Miss—er—Mitchell," Lincoln Creed said. "It's cold and getting colder, and it'll be dark soon. I didn't see a rig outside, so I figure you must have walked to town. I've got my team and buckboard outside, and I'd be glad to give you and those kids a ride to wherever you're headed."

Tears welled in Juliana's eyes, shaming her, and her throat tightened painfully. Wherever she was headed? *Nowhere* was where she was headed.

Stillwater Springs had a hotel and several boarding houses, but even if she'd had the wherewithal to pay for a room and meals, most likely none of them would have accepted the children, anyway.

They'd hurried so, trying to get to Stillwater Springs before the train left, Juliana desperately counting on the funds from Clay even against her better judgment, but there had been delays. Little Daisy falling and skinning one knee, a huge band of sheep crossing the road and blocking their way, the limp that plagued twelve-year-old Theresa, with her twisted foot.

Lincoln broke into her thoughts. "Miss Mitchell?" he prompted.

Mr. Willand slammed something down hard on the counter, causing Juliana to start. "Don't you touch none of that merchandise!" he shouted, and Joseph, the eldest of Juliana's pupils at fourteen, pulled his hand back from the display window. "Damn thievin' Injuns—"

Poor Joseph looked crestfallen. Theresa, his sister, trembled, while the two littlest children, Billy-Moses, who was four, and Daisy, three, rushed to Juliana and clung to her skirts in fear.

"The boy wasn't doing any harm, Fred," Lincoln told the storekeeper evenly, rising slowly out of his chair. "No need to raise your voice, or accuse him, either."

Mr. Willand reddened. "You have a grocery order?" he asked, glowering at Lincoln Creed.

"Just came by to see if I had mail," Lincoln said, with a shake of his head. "Couldn't get here before now, what with the hard weather coming on." He paused, turned to Juliana. "Best we get you to wherever it is you're going," he said.

"We don't have anyplace to go, mister," Joseph said, still standing near the display window, but careful to keep his hands visible at his sides. Since he rarely spoke, especially to strangers, Juliana was startled.

And as desperate as she was, the words chafed her pride.

Lincoln frowned, obviously confused. "What?"

"They might take us in over at the Diamond Buckle Saloon," Theresa said, lifting her chin. "If we work for our keep."

Lincoln stared at the girl, confounded. "The Diamond Buckle…?"

Juliana didn't trust herself to speak without breaking down completely. If she did not remain strong, the children would have no hope at all.

"Mr. Weston Creed said he'd teach me to set type," Joseph reminded Juliana. "Bet I could sleep in the back room at the newspaper, and I don't need much to eat. You wouldn't have to fret about me, Miss Mitchell." He glanced worriedly at his sister, swallowed hard. He was old enough to understand the dangers a place like the Diamond Buckle might harbor for a young girl, even if Theresa wasn't.

Lincoln raised both hands, palms out, in a bid for silence.

Everyone stared at him, including Juliana, who had pulled little Daisy onto her lap.

"All of you," Lincoln said, addressing the children, "gather up whatever things you've got and get into the back of my buckboard. You'll find some blankets there—wrap up warm, because it's three miles to the ranch house and there's an icy wind blowing in from the northwest."

Juliana stood, gently displacing Daisy, careful to keep the child close against her side. "Mr. Creed, we couldn't accept…" Her voice fell away, and mortification burned in her cheeks.

"Seems to me," Lincoln said, "you don't have much of a choice. I'm offering you and these children a place to stay, Miss Mitchell. Just till you can figure out what to do next."

"You'd let these savages set foot under the same roof with your little Gracie?" Mr. Willand blustered, incensed. He'd crossed the otherwise-empty store, shouldered Joseph aside to peer into the display window and make sure nothing was missing.

The air pulsed again.

Lincoln took a step toward the storekeeper.

By instinct, Juliana grasped Mr. Creed's arm to stop him. Even through the heavy fabric of his coat, she could feel that his muscles were steely with tension—he was barely containing his temper. "The children are used to remarks like that," she said quietly, anxious to keep the peace. "They know they aren't savages."

"Get into the wagon," Lincoln said. He didn't pull free of Juliana's touch, nor did he look away from Mr. Willand's crimson face. "All of you."

The children looked to Juliana, their dark, luminous eyes liquid with wary question.

She nodded, silently giving her permission.

Almost as one, they scrambled for the door, causing the bell to clamor merrily overhead. Even Daisy, clinging until a moment before, peeled away from Juliana's side.

After pulling her cloak more closely around her and raising the hood against the cold wind, Juliana followed.

LINCOLN WATCHED THEM GO. He'd hung his hat on one of the spindle-backed wooden chairs next to the stove earlier, and he reached for it. "There's enough grief and sorrow in this world," he told the storekeeper, "without folks like you adding to it."

Willand was undaunted, though Lincoln noticed he stayed well behind the counter, within bolting distance of the back door. "We'll see what *Mrs.* Creed says, when you turn up on her doorstep with a tribe of Injuns—"

Lincoln shoved his hat down on top of his head with a little more force than the effort required. His wife, Beth, had died two years before, of a fever, so Willand was referring to his mother. Cora Creed would indeed have been surprised to find five extra people seated around her supper table that night—if Lincoln hadn't left her with enough bags to fill a freight car at the train depot before stopping by the mercantile. She was headed for Phoenix, where she liked to winter with her kinfolks, the Dawsons.

"I'll be back tomorrow if I get the chance," he said, starting for the door. With that storm coming and cattle to feed, he couldn't be sure. "To see if any letters came in on today's train."

Willand glanced at the big regulator clock on the wall behind him. "My boy's gone to the depot, like always, and he'll be here with the mail bag any minute now," he said grudgingly. "Might as well wait."

Lincoln went to the window, looked past his own reflection in the darkening glass—God, he hated the shortness of winter days—to see Miss Mitchell settling her unlikely brood in the bed of his wagon. Something warmed inside him, shifted. The slightest smile tilted one corner of his mouth.

He'd been advertising for a governess for his seven-year-old daughter, Gracie, and a housekeeper for the both of them for nearly a year; failing either of those, he'd settle for a wife, and because he knew he'd never love another woman the way he'd loved Beth, he wasn't too choosey in his requirements.

Juliana Mitchell, with her womanly figure, indigo-blue eyes and those tendrils of coppery hair peeking out from under her worn bonnet, was clearly dedicated to her profession, since she'd stayed to look after those children even now that the Indian School had closed down. A lot of schoolmarms wouldn't have done that.

This spoke well for her character, and when it came to looks, she was a better bargain than anyone all those advertisements might have scared up.

Glancing down at the display, with all the toys Willand was hoping to sell before Christmas, Lincoln's gaze fell on the corner of a metal box, tucked at an odd angle under the bunting beneath the tree. He reached for the item, drew it out, saw that it was a set of watercolor paints, similar to one Gracie had at home.

Was this what the boy had been looking at when Willand pitched a fit?

For reasons he couldn't have explained, Lincoln was sure it was.

He held the long, flat tin up for Willand to see, before tucking it into the inside pocket of his coat. "Put this on my bill," he said.

Willand grumbled, but a sale was a sale. He finally nodded.

Lincoln raised his collar against the cold and left the mercantile for the wooden sidewalk beyond.

The kids were settled in the back of the wagon, all but the oldest boy snuggled in the rough woolen blankets Lincoln always carried in winter. Juliana Mitchell waited primly on the seat, straight-spined, chin high, trying not to shiver in that thin cloak of hers.

Buttoning his coat as he left the store, Lincoln unbuttoned it again before climbing up into the box beside her. Snowflakes drifted slowly from a gray sky as he took up the reins, released the brake lever. The streets of the town were nearly deserted—folks were getting ready for the storm, feeling its approach in their bones, just as Lincoln did.

Knowing her pride would make her balk if he took off his coat and put it around her, he pulled his right arm out of the sleeve and drew her to his side instead, closing the garment around her.

She stiffened, then went still, in what he guessed was resignation.

It bruised something inside Lincoln, realizing how

many things Juliana Mitchell had probably had to resign herself to over the course of her life.

He set the team in motion, kept his gaze on the snowy road ahead, winding toward home. By the time they reached the ranch, it would be dark out, but the horses knew their way.

Meanwhile, Juliana Mitchell felt warm and soft against him. He'd forgotten what it was like to protect a woman, shield her against his side, and the remembrance was painful, like frostbitten flesh beginning to thaw.

Beth had been gone awhile, and though he wasn't proud of it, in the last six months or so he'd turned to loose women for comfort a time or two, over in Choteau or in Missoula.

The quickening he felt now was different, of course. Though anybody could see she was down on her luck, it was equally obvious that Juliana Mitchell was a lady. Breeding was a thing even shabby clothes couldn't hide—especially from a rancher used to raising fine cattle and horses.

Minutes later, as they jostled over the road in the buckboard, Juliana relaxed against Lincoln, and it came to him, with a flash of amusement, that she was asleep.

Plainly, she was exhausted. From the way her face had fallen as she'd read that letter, which she'd finally wadded up and stuffed into the pocket of her cloak with an expression of heartbroken disgust in her eyes, she'd suffered some bitter disappointment.

All he knew for sure was that nobody had died, since he'd asked her that right off.

Lincoln tried to imagine what kind of news might have thrown her like that, even though he knew it was none of his business.

Maybe she'd planned to marry the man who'd written that letter, and he'd spurned her for another.

Lincoln frowned, aware of the woman's softness and warmth in every part of his lonesome body. What kind of damned fool would do that?

His shoulder began to ache, since his arm was curved around Juliana at a somewhat awkward angle, but he didn't care. He'd have driven right past the ranch, just so she could go on resting against him like that for a little while longer, if he hadn't been a practical man.

The wind picked up, and the snow came down harder and faster, and when he looked back at the kids, they were sitting stoically in their places, bundled in their blankets.

The best part of an hour had passed when the lights of the ranch house finally came into view, glowing dim and golden in the snow-swept darkness.

Lincoln's heartbeat picked up a little, the way it always did when he rounded that last bend in the road and saw home waiting up ahead.

Home.

He'd been born in the rambling, one-story log house, with its stone chimneys, the third son of Josiah and Cora Creed. Micah, the firstborn, had long since left the ranch, started a place of his own down in Colorado. Weston, the next in line, lived in town, in rooms above the Diamond Buckle Saloon, and published the *Courier*—when he was sober enough to run the presses.

Two years younger than Wes, Lincoln had left home only to attend college in Boston and apprentice himself to a lawyer—Beth's father. As soon as he was qualified to practice, Lincoln had married Beth, brought her home to Stillwater Springs Ranch and loved her with all the passion a man could feel for a woman.

She'd taken to life on a remote Montana ranch with amazing acuity for a city girl, and if she'd missed Boston, she'd never once let on. She'd given him Gracie, and they'd been happy.

Now she rested in the small, sad cemetery beyond the apple orchard, like Josiah, and the fourth Creed brother, Dawson.

Dawson. Sometimes it was harder to think about him and the way he'd died, than to recall Beth succumbing to that fever.

Juliana straightened against Lincoln's side, yawned. If the darkness hadn't hidden her face, the brim of her bonnet would have, but he sensed that she was embarrassed by the lapse.

"We're almost home," he said, just loudly enough for her to hear.

She didn't answer, but sat up a little straighter, wanting to pull away, but confined by his arm and the cloth of his coat.

When they reached the gate with its overarching sign, Lincoln moved to get down, but the Indian boy, Joseph, was faster. He worked the latch, swung the gate wide, and Lincoln drove the buckboard through.

His father and Tom Dancingstar had cut and planed the timber for that sign, chiseled the letters into it, and then laboriously deepened them with pokers heated in the homemade forge they'd used for horseshoeing.

Lincoln never saw the words without a feeling of quiet gratification and pride.

Stillwater Springs Ranch.

He held the team while the boy shut the gate, then scrambled back into the wagon. The horses were eager to get to the barn, where hay and water and warm stalls awaited them.

Tom was there to help unhitch the team when Lincoln drove through the wide doorway and under the sturdy barn roof. Part Lakota Sioux, part Cherokee and part devil by his own accounting, Tom had worked on the ranch from the beginning. He'd named himself, claiming no white tongue could manage the handle he'd been given at birth.

He smiled when he saw Juliana, and she smiled back. Clearly, they were acquainted.

Was he, Lincoln wondered, the only yahoo in the countryside who'd never met the teacher from the Indian School?

"Take the kids inside the house," Lincoln told Juliana, and it struck him that rather than the strangers they were, they might have been married for years, the two of them, all these children their own. "Tom and I will be in as soon as we've finished here."

He paused to lift the two smaller children out of the wagon; sleepy-eyed, still wrapped in their blankets, they stumbled a little, befuddled to find themselves in a barn lit by lanterns, surrounded by horses and Jenny Lind, the milk cow.

"I'll tend to the horses," Tom told him. "There's a kettle of stew warming on the stove, and Gracie's been watching the road for you since sunset."

Thinking of his gold-haired, blue-eyed daughter, Lincoln smiled. Smarter than three judges and as many juries put together, Gracie tended toward fretfulness. Losing her mother when she was only five caused her to worry about him whenever he was out of her sight.

With a ranch the size of his to run, he was away from the house a lot, accustomed to leaving the child in the care of his now-absent mother, or Rose-of-Sharon Gainer, the cumbersomely pregnant young wife of one of the ranch hands.

The older boy's gaze had fastened on Tom.

"Can I stay here and help?" he asked.

"May I," Juliana corrected with a smile. "Yes, Joseph, you may."

With that, she leaned down, weary as she was, and lifted the littlest girl into her arms. Lincoln bent to hoist up the smaller boy.

"This is Daisy," Juliana told him. "That's Billy-Moses you're holding." The girl who'd spoken of working for her keep at the Diamond Buckle ducked her head shyly, stood a little closer to her teacher. "And this is Theresa," she finished.

Leaving Tom and Joseph to put the team up for the night, Lincoln shed his coat at the entrance to the barn, draped it over Juliana's shoulders. It dragged on the snowy ground, and she smiled wanly at that, hiking the garment up with her free arm, closing it around both herself and Daisy.

They entered the house by the side door, stepping into the warmth, the aroma of Tom's venison stew and the light of several lanterns. Gracie, rocking in the chair near the cookstove and pretending she hadn't been waiting impatiently for Lincoln's return, went absolutely still when she saw that he wasn't alone.

Her cornflower-blue eyes widened, and her mouth made a perfect O.

Daisy and Billy-Moses stared back at her, probably as amazed as she was.

"Gracie," Lincoln said unnecessarily. "We have company."

Gracie had recovered by then; she fairly leaped out of the rocking chair. Looking up at Juliana, she asked, "Did you answer one of my papa's advertisements? Are you going to be a governess, a housekeeper or a wife?"

Lincoln winced.

Understandably, Juliana seemed taken aback. Like Gracie, though, she turned out to be pretty resilient. The only sign that the child's question had caught her off guard was the faint tinge of pink beneath her cheekbones, and that might have been from the cold.

"I'm Miss Mitchell," she said kindly. "These are my pupils—Daisy, Billy-Moses and Theresa. There's Joseph, as well—he's out in the barn helping Mr. Dancingstar look after the horses."

"Then you're a *governess!*" Gracie cried jubilantly. Young as she was, she could already read, and because Lincoln wouldn't allow her to travel back and forth to school in Stillwater Springs, she was convinced that lifelong ignorance would be her lot.

"Gracie," Lincoln said, setting Billy-Moses on his feet. "Miss Mitchell is a guest. She didn't answer any advertisements."

Gracie looked profoundly disappointed, but only for a moment. Like most Creeds, when she set her mind on something, she did not give up easily.

For the next little while, they were all busy with supper.

Tom and Joseph came in from the barn, pumped water at the sink to wash up and joined them at the table, while Gracie, who had already eaten, rushed about fetching bread and butter and ladling milk from the big covered crock stored on the back step.

His daughter wanted to make Miss Mitchell feel welcome, Lincoln thought with a smile, so she'd stay and teach her all she wanted to know—and that was considerable. She hadn't asked for a doll for Christmas, or a spinning top, like a lot of little girls would have done.

Oh, no. Gracie wanted a dictionary.

Wes often joked that by the time his niece was old enough to make the trip to town on her own, she'd be half again too smart for school and ready to take over the

Courier so he could spend the rest of his life smoking cigars and playing poker.

As far as Lincoln could tell, his brother did little else but smoke cigars and play poker—not counting, of course, the whiskey-swilling and his long-standing and wholly scandalous love affair with Kate Winthrop, who happened to own the Diamond Buckle.

Gracie adored her uncle Weston—and Kate.

Casting a surreptitious glance in Juliana's direction whenever he could during supper, Lincoln saw that she could barely keep her eyes open. As soon as the meal was over, he showed her to his mother's spacious room. She and Daisy and Billy-Moses could share the big feather bed.

Joseph bunked in with Tom, who slept in a small chamber behind the kitchen stove, having given up his cabin out by the bunkhouse to Ben Gainer and his wife. Theresa was to sleep with Gracie.

Lincoln's young daughter, however, was not in bed. Wide-awake, she sat at the table with Lincoln, watching as he drank lukewarm coffee, left over from earlier in the day.

"Go to bed, Gracie," he told her.

Tom lingered by the stove, also drinking coffee. He smiled when Gracie didn't move.

"I couldn't possibly sleep," she said seriously. "I am entirely too excited."

Lincoln sighed. She was knee-high to a fence post, but sometimes she talked like someone her grandmother's age. "It's still five days until Christmas," he reminded her. "Too soon to be all het up over presents and such."

"I'm not excited about *Christmas,*" Gracie said, with the exaggerated patience she might have shown the village idiot. Stillwater Springs boasted its share of those. "You're going to marry Miss Mitchell, and I'll have Billy-Moses and Daisy to play with—"

Tom chuckled into his coffee cup.

Lincoln sighed again and settled back in his chair. Although he'd thought about hitching up with the schoolteacher, he'd probably been hasty. "Gracie, Miss Mitchell isn't here to marry me. She was stranded in town because the Indian School closed down, so I brought her and the kids home—"

"Will I still have to call her 'Miss Mitchell' after you get married to her? She'd be 'Mrs. Creed' then, wouldn't she? It would be really silly for me to go around saying 'Mrs. Creed' all the time—"

"Gracie."

"What?"

"Go to bed."

"I told you, I'm too excited."

"And *I* told *you* to go to bed."

"Oh, for heaven's sake," Gracie protested, disgruntled.

But she got out of her chair at the table, said good-night to Tom and stood on tiptoe to kiss Lincoln on the cheek.

His heart melted like a honeycomb under a hot sun when she did that. Her blue eyes, so like Beth's, sparkled as she looked up at him, then turned solemn.

"Be nice to Miss Mitchell, Papa," she instructed solemnly. "Stand up when she comes into a room, and pull her chair back for her. We want her to like it here and stay."

Lincoln's throat constricted, and his eyes burned. He couldn't have answered to save his hide from a hot brand.

"You'll come and hear my prayers?" Gracie asked, the way she did every night.

The prayers varied slightly, but certain parts were always the same.

Please keep my papa safe, and Tom, too. I'd like a dog of my very own, one that will fetch, and I want to go to school, so I don't grow up to be stupid....

Lincoln nodded his assent. Though it was a request he never refused, Gracie always asked.

Once she left the room, Tom set his cup in the sink, folded his arms. "According to young Joseph," he said, "he and his sister have folks in North Dakota—an aunt and a grandfather. Soon as he can save enough money, he means to head for home and take Theresa with him."

Lincoln felt a lot older than his thirty-five years as he raised himself from his chair, began turning down lamp wicks, one by one. Tom, in the meantime, banked the fire in the cookstove.

They were usual, these long gaps in their conversations. Right or wrong, Lincoln had always been closer to Tom than to his own father—Josiah Creed had been a hard man in many ways. Neither Lincoln nor Wes had mourned him overmuch—they left that to Micah, the eldest, and their mother.

"Did the boy happen to say how he and the girl wound up in a school outside of Stillwater Springs, Montana?"

Tom straightened, his profile grim in the last of the lantern light. "The government decided he and his sister would be better off if they learned white ways," he said. "Took them off the reservation in North Dakota a couple of years ago, and they were in several different 'institutions' before their luck changed. They haven't seen their people since the day they left Dakota, though Juliana helped him write a letter to them six months back, and they got an answer." Tom paused, swallowed visibly. His voice sounded hoarse. "The folks at home want them back, Lincoln."

Lincoln stood in the relative darkness for a few moments, reflecting. "I'll send them, then," he said after a long time. "Put them on the train when it comes through next week."

Tom didn't answer immediately, and when he did, the whole Trail of Tears echoed in his voice. "They're just kids. They oughtn't to make a trip like that alone."

Another lengthy silence rested comfortably between the two men. Then Lincoln said, "You want to go with them."

"Somebody ought to," Tom replied. "Make sure they get there all right. Might be that things have changed since that letter came."

Lincoln absorbed that, finally nodded. "What about the little ones?" he asked without looking at his friend. "Daisy and Billy-Moses?"

"They're orphans," Tom said, and sadness settled over the darkened room like a weight. "Reckon Miss

Mitchell planned on keeping them until she could find them a home."

Lincoln sighed inwardly. *Until she could find them a home.* As if those near-babies were stray puppies or kittens.

With another nod, this one sorrowful, he turned away.

It was time to turn in; morning would come early.

But damned if he'd sleep a wink between the plight of four innocent children and the knowledge that Juliana Mitchell was lying on the other side of the wall.

Chapter Two

The mattress felt like a cloud, tufted and stuffed with feathers from angels' wings, beneath Juliana's weary frame, but sleep eluded her. Daisy slumbered innocently at her right side, sucking one tiny thumb, while Billy-Moses snuggled close on the left, clinging to her flannel nightgown—the cloth was still chilled from being rolled up in her satchel, out in the weather most of the day.

Juliana listened as the sturdy house settled around her, her body still stiff with tension, that being its long-established habit, heard a plank creaking here, a roof timber there. She caught the sound of a door opening and closing just down the corridor, pictured Lincoln Creed passing into his room, or bending over little Gracie's bed to tuck her in and bid her good-night. Would he spare a kind word for Theresa, who was sharing Gracie's room, and so hungry for affection, or reserve all his attention for his little daughter?

Gracie was a charming child, as lovely as a doll come to life, with those thickly lashed eyes, golden ringlets brushing her shoulders and the pink-tinged porcelain perfection of her skin. Privileged by comparison to most children, not to mention the four in Juliana's own charge, Gracie was precocious, but if she was spoiled, there had been no sign of it yet. She'd greeted the new arrivals at Stillwater Springs Ranch with frank curiosity, yes, but then she'd ladled milk into mugs for them, even served it at the table.

Juliana's heart pinched. Gracie had a strong, loving father, a home, robust good health. But behind those more obvious blessings lurked a certain lonely resignation uncommon in one so young. Gracie had lost her mother at a very early age, and no one understood the sorrows of that more than Juliana herself—she'd been six years old when her own had succumbed to consumption. Juliana's father, outraged by grief, torn asunder by it, had dumped both his offspring on their maternal grandmother's doorstep barely two weeks after his wife's funeral and, over the next few years, delivered himself up to dissolution and debauchery.

Clay, nine at the time of their mother's passing, had changed from a lighthearted, mischievous boy to a solemn-faced man, seemingly overnight. In a very real way, Juliana had lost him, in addition to both her parents.

Victoria Marston, their grandmother, already a widow when her only daughter had died, dressed in mourning until her own death a decade later, but she had loved Juliana and Clay tirelessly nonetheless. Grandmama had given them every advantage—tutors, music lessons, finishing school for Juliana, who had immediately changed the course of her study to train as a schoolteacher upon the discovery that "finishing" involved learning to make small talk with men, the proper way to pour tea and a lot of walking about with a book balanced on top of her head. There had been college in San Francisco for Clay, even a Grand Tour.

Juliana had stayed behind in Denver, living at home

with Grandmama, attending classes every day and letting her doting grandmother believe she was being thoroughly "finished," impatiently waiting for her life to begin.

For all the things she would have changed, she appreciated her blessings, too; she'd been well-cared-for, beautifully clothed and educated beyond the level most young women attained. Yet, there was still a childlike yearning inside Juliana, a longing for her beautiful, laughing mama. The singular and often poignant ache was mostly manageable—except when she was discouraged, and that had been often, of late.

After graduating from Normal School—her grandmother had died of a heart condition only weeks before Juliana accepted her certificate—she'd begun her career with high hopes, pushed up her sleeves and flung herself into the fray, undaunted at first by her brother's cold disapproval. He'd wanted her to marry his business partner, John Holden, and because he controlled their grandmother's large estate, Clay had had the power to disinherit her. On the day she'd given back John's engagement ring and accepted her first teaching assignment at a school for Indian boys in a small Colorado town a day's train ride from Denver, he'd done that, for all practical intents and purposes.

Juliana had been left with nothing but the few modest clothes and personal belongings she'd packed for the journey. Clay had gone so far as to ban her from the family home, saying she could return when she "came to her senses."

To Clay, "coming to her senses" meant consigning herself to a loveless marriage to a widower more than twenty years her senior, a man with two daughters close to Juliana's own age.

Mean daughters, who went out of their way to be snide, and saw their future stepmother as an interloper bent on claiming their late mother's jewelry, as well as her home and husband.

Remembering, Juliana bit down on her lower lip, and her eyes smarted a little. She might have been content with John, if not happy, had it not been for Eleanor and Eugenie. He was gentle, well-read, and she'd felt safe with him.

In a flash of insight and dismay, Juliana had realized she was looking for a father, not a husband. She'd explained to John, and though he'd been disappointed, he'd understood. He'd even been gracious enough to wish her well.

Clay, by contrast, had been furious; his otherwise

handsome features had turned to stone the day she'd told him about the broken engagement.

In the six years since, he'd softened a little—probably because his wife, Nora, had lobbied steadily on Juliana's behalf—writing regularly, even inviting Juliana home for visits and offering to ship the clothing and books she'd left behind, but when it came to her inheritance, he'd never relented.

Even when John Holden had died suddenly, a year before, permanently disqualifying himself as a possible husband for the sister Clay had once adored and protected, teased and laughed with, he had not given ground. After months of working up her courage, she'd written to ask for a modest bank draft, since her salary was small, less than the allowance her grandmother had given her as a girl, and Clay had responded with words that still blistered Juliana's pride, even now. "I won't see you squandering good money," he'd written, "on shoes and schoolbooks for a pack of red-skinned orphans and strays."

A burning ache rose in Juliana's throat at the memory.

Clay would cease punishing her when she stopped teaching and married a man who met with his lofty approval, then and only then, and that was the unfortunate reality.

She'd been a fool to write to him that last time, all but begging for the funds she'd needed to get Joseph and Theresa safely home to North Dakota and look after the two little ones until proper homes could be found for them.

The situation was further complicated by the fact that Mr. Philbert, an agent of the Bureau of Indian Affairs and therefore Juliana's supervisor, believed the four pupils still in her charge had been sent back to their original school in Missoula, along with the older students. Sooner or later, making his rounds or by correspondence, Philbert, a diligent sort with no softness in him that Juliana could discern, would realize she'd not only disobeyed his orders, but lied to him, at least in part.

As an official representative of the United States government, the man could have her arrested and prosecuted for kidnapping, and consign Daisy and Billy-Moses to some new institution, far out of her reach, where they would probably be neglected, at best. Juliana knew, after working in a series of such places, all but bloodying her very soul in the effort to change things, that only the most dedicated reformers would bother to look beyond the color of their skin. And there were precious few of those.

To keep from thinking about Mr. Philbert and his inevitable wrath, Juliana turned her mind to the students she'd had to bid farewell to—Mary Rose, seventeen and soon to be entering Normal School herself; Ezekiel, sixteen, who wanted to finish his education and return to his tribe. Finally, there was Angelique, seventeen, like her cousin Mary Rose, sweet and unassuming and smitten with a boy she'd met while running an errand in Stillwater Springs one spring day.

Part Blackfoot and part white, Blue Johnston had visited several times, a handsome, engaging young man with a flashing white smile and the promise of a job herding cattle on a ranch outside of Missoula. Although Juliana had kept close watch on the couple and warned Angelique repeatedly about the perils of impulse, she'd had the other children to attend to, and the pair had strayed out of her sight more than a few times.

Privately, Juliana feared that Angelique and her beau would run away and get married as soon as they got the chance—and that chance had come a week before, when Angelique and the others had boarded the train to return to Missoula. Should that happen—perhaps it already had—Mr. Philbert would bluster and threaten dire consequences when he learned of it, all the while figuratively dusting his hands together, secretly relieved to have one less obligation.

Footsteps passed along the hallway, past her door, bringing Juliana out of her rueful reflections. Another door opened and then closed again, nearer, and then all was silent.

The house rested, and so, evidently, did Lincoln Creed.

Juliana could not.

Easing herself from between the sleeping children, after gently freeing the fabric of her nightgown from Billy-Moses's grasp, Juliana crawled out of bed.

The cold slammed against her body like the shock following an explosion; there was a small stove in the room, but it had not been lit.

Shivering, Juliana crossed to it, all but hopping, found matches and newspaper and kindling and larger chunks of pitchy wood resting tidily in a nearby basket. With numb fingers, she opened the stove door and laid a fire, set the newspaper and kindling ablaze, adjusted the damper.

The floor stung the soles of her bare feet, and the

single window, though large, was opaque with curlicues and crystals of ice. A silvery glow indicated that the moon had come out from behind the snow-burdened clouds—perhaps the storm had stopped.

Juliana paced, making no sound, until the room began to warm up, and then fumbled in the pocket of her cloak for Clay's crumpled letter. Back at the mercantile, she'd been too overwrought to finish the missive. Now, wakeful in the house of a charitable stranger—but a stranger nevertheless—she smoothed the page with the flat of one hand, hungry for a word of kind affection.

Not wanting to light a lamp, lest she awaken the children resting so soundly in the feather bed, Juliana knelt near the fire, opened the stove door again and read by the flickering flames inside, welcoming the warmth.

Her gaze skimmed over the first few lines—she could have recited those from memory—and took in the rest.

You will be twenty-six years old on your next birthday, Juliana, and you are still unmarried. Nora and I are, of course, greatly concerned for your welfare, not to mention your reputation....

Juliana had to stop herself by the summoning of inner forces from wadding the letter up again, casting it straight into the fire.

Clay had accepted the fact, he continued, in his usual brisk fashion, that his sister had consigned herself to a life of lonely and wasteful spinsterhood. She was creating a scandal, he maintained, by living away from home and family. What kind of example, he wondered, was she setting for Clara, her little niece?

He closed with what amounted to a command that she return to Denver and "live with modesty and circumspection" in her brother's home, where she belonged.

But there was no expression of fondness.

The letter was signed *Regards, C. Mitchell.*

"'C. Mitchell,'" Juliana whispered on a shaky breath. "Not 'Clay.' Not 'Your brother.' 'C. Mitchell.'"

With that, she folded the single page carefully, held it for a moment, and then tossed it into the stove. Watched, the heat drying her eyeballs until they burned, as orange flames curled the vellum, nibbled darkly at the edges and corners, and then consumed the last forlorn tatters of Juliana's hopes. There would be no reconciliation between her and Clay, no restoration of their old childhood camaraderie.

As much as she had loved the brother she remembered from long ago, as much as she loved him still, for surely he was still in there somewhere behind that rigid facade, she *could not* go home. Oh, she would have enjoyed getting to know little Clara and her brother, Simon. She had always been fond of Nora, a good-hearted if flighty woman who accepted her husband's absolute authority without apparent qualms. But Clay would treat her, Juliana, like a poor relation, doling out pennies for a packet of pins, lecturing and dictating her every move, staring her down if she dared to venture an opinion at the supper table.

No. She definitely could not go home, not under such circumstances. It would be the ultimate—and final—defeat, and the slow death of her spirit.

"Missy?" The lisp was Daisy's; the child could not say Juliana's whole name, and always addressed her thus. "Missy, are you there?"

"I'm here, sweetheart," Juliana confirmed quietly, closing the stove door and getting back to her feet. "I'm here."

The assurance was enough for Daisy; she turned onto her side, settled in with a tiny murmur of relief and sank into sleep again.

Even with the fire going, the room was still cold enough to numb Juliana's bones.

Having no other choice, she climbed back into bed and pulled the top sheet and faded quilts up to her chin, giving a little shiver.

Billy-Moses stirred beside her, took a new hold on her nightgown.

Daisy snuggled close, too.

Juliana stared up at the ceiling, watching the shadows dance, her heart and mind crowded with children again. At some point, she could send Joseph and Theresa home by train to their family in North Dakota.

But what of Daisy and Billy-Moses? They had nowhere to go, besides an orphanage or some other "school."

In her more optimistic moments, Juliana could convince herself that some kindly couple would be delighted to adopt these bright, beautiful children, would cherish and nurture them.

This was not an optimistic moment.

Poverty was rampant among Indians; many could not

feed their own children, let alone take in the lost lambs, the "strays," as Clay and others like him referred to them.

A lone tear slipped down Juliana's right cheek, tickled its way over her temple and into her hair. She closed her eyes and waited, trying not to consider the future, and finally, fitfully, she slept.

THE COLD WAS BRITTLE; it had substance and heft.

Lincoln had carried in an armload of wood and laid kindling on the hearth of the big stone fireplace directly across from his too-big, too-empty four-poster bed that morning before dawn, the way he always did after the weather turned in the fall. He'd gotten a good blaze crackling in the little stove in Gracie's room, so she and Theresa would be snug—he'd seen children sicken and die after taking a chill—but that night he didn't bother to get his own fire going.

He stripped off his clothes and the long winter underwear beneath them, and plunged into bed naked, cursing under his breath at the smooth, icy bite of the linen sheets. It was at night that he generally missed Beth most, recalling her whispery laughter and the warmth of her curled against him, the sweet, eager solace of their lovemaking.

Tonight, it was different.

He couldn't stop thinking about Juliana: her new-penny hair; her eyes, blue as wet ink pooling on the whitest paper; the way she'd rested against his side, under his coat, soft with the innocent abandon of sleep, on the wagon ride home from town.

He reckoned that was why he wouldn't light a fire. He was punishing himself for betraying Beth's memory in a way that cut far deeper than relieving his body with dance-hall girls in other towns. God Almighty, he'd had to study the little gilt-framed picture of his late wife on Gracie's night table earlier just to reassemble her features in his mind. They'd scattered like dry leaves in a high wind, the memory of Beth's eyes and nose and the shape of her mouth, with his first look at Juliana that afternoon, in the mercantile.

Beth would have understood about the loose women.

Even a mail-order bride.

But he'd vowed, sitting beside this very bed, holding Beth's hand in both his own, to love her, and no one else, until they laid him out in the cemetery alongside her.

Lincoln's eyes stung as he remembered how brave she'd been. How she'd smiled at his earnest promise, sick as she was, and told him not to close his heart, for Gracie's sake and his own.

She hadn't meant it, of course. She'd read a lot of novels about love and chivalry and noble sacrifice, that was all. A woman of comparatively few flaws, at least as far as he was concerned, Beth had nonetheless been possessive at times, her jealousy flaring when he tipped his hat to any female under the age of sixty, or returned a smile.

He'd been faithful, besotted as he was, but Beth's wealthy father had kept a mistress while she was growing up, and her mother had withdrawn into bitter silence in protest, becoming an invalid by choice. Though the instances were rare, Beth had fretted and shed tears a time or two, certain that it was only a matter of time before Lincoln tired of her and wanted some conjugal variety.

He'd reassured her, of course, kissed away her tears, made love to her, sent away to cities like New York and San Francisco and Boston for small but expensive presents he hadn't been able to afford, what with beef prices bottoming out and his mother spending money as if she still had a rich husband, and his brother Wes running the ranch into near bankruptcy while he, Lincoln, was away at college.

No, he thought, with a shake of his head and a grim set to his mouth, his hands cupped behind his head as he lay still as fallen timber, waiting for the sheets to warm up. Beth hadn't meant what she'd said that day, only hours before she'd closed her eyes for the last time; she'd merely been playing out a scene from one of those stories that made her sniffle until her face got puffy and her nose turned red. She'd believed, being so very young, that that was how a lady was supposed to die.

If it hadn't been for the seizing ache in the middle of his chest and the sting behind his eyes, Lincoln might have smiled to remember the earlier days of their marriage, when he'd come in from the barn or the range so many evenings and found his bride with a thick book clutched to her bosom and tears pouring down her cheeks.

"She died with a rose clasped between her teeth!" Beth had expounded once, evidently referring to the heroine of the novel she'd been reading by the front room fire.

His mother, darning socks in her rocking chair, wanting them both to know she disapproved of such nonsense, and saucy brides from Somewhere Else, had muttered something, shaken her head and then made a tsk-tsk sound.

"*Someone* had better start supper cooking," Cora Creed had huffed, rising and stalking off toward the kitchen.

Waited on by servants all her short life, Beth had never learned to cook, sew or even make up a bed. None of that had bothered Lincoln, though it troubled his mother plenty.

He had merely smiled, kissed Beth's overheated forehead and said something along the lines of "I hope she was careful not to bite down on the thorns. The lady in the book, I mean."

Beth had laughed then, and hit him playfully with the tome.

Now, alone in the bed where they'd conceived Gracie and two other children who hadn't survived long enough to draw even one breath, Lincoln thrust out a sigh and rubbed his eyes with a thumb and forefinger.

Morning would come around early, and the day ahead would be long, hard and cold. He and Tom and the few ranch hands wintering on the place would be hauling wagonloads of hay out to the range cattle, since the grass was buried under snow. They'd have to break the ice at the edge of the creek, too, so the cattle could drink.

He needed whatever sleep he could get.

Plainly, it wouldn't be much.

JULIANA HAD BEEN an early riser since the cradle, and she was up and dressed well before dawn.

Even so, when she wandered through the still-dark house toward the kitchen, there was a blaze burning in the hearth in what probably passed for a parlor in such a masculine home. The furniture was heavy and dark and spare, all hard leather and rough-hewn wood, the surfaces uncluttered with the usual knickknacks and vases and doilies and sewing baskets.

Perhaps Lincoln's mother—gone traveling, Gracie had said at supper, with marked relief—had packed away her things in preparation for a lengthy absence. As far as Juliana could tell, the woman had left no trace at all—even her room, where she and the children had passed the night, was unadorned.

Entering the kitchen, Juliana stepped into lantern-light and the warmth of the cookstove. Lincoln stood at a basin in front of a small mirror fixed to the wall, his face lathered with suds, shaving. He wore trousers and boots and a long-sleeved woolen undershirt, and suspenders that dangled in loose, manly loops at his sides.

He was decently clothed, but there was an intimacy in the early-morning quiet and the glow of the kerosene lamps that gave Juliana pause. She stopped on the threshold and drew in a sharp breath.

He smiled, rinsed his straight razor in the basin, ran it skillfully under his chin and along his neck. "Mornin'," he said.

Juliana recovered her inner composure, but barely. "Good morning," she replied, quite formally.

"Coffee's ready," Lincoln told her. "Help yourself. Cups are on the shelf in the pantry." He cocked a thumb toward a nearby door.

Juliana hurried in to get a cup, desperate to be busy. Came back with two, since that was the polite thing to do. She poured coffee for Lincoln, started to take it to him and was suddenly tongue-tied again, and flustered by it.

He chuckled, rinsed his face in the basin, reached for a towel and dried off. His ebony hair was rumpled, and glossy in the lamplight. "Thanks," he said, and walked over to take the steaming cup from her hand.

Tom entered while they were standing there, staring at each other, his bronzed skin polished with the cold. Behind him walked Joseph, carrying a bucket steaming with fresh milk.

Juliana smiled, feeling as though she'd been rescued

from something intriguingly dangerous. "You're up early," she said to the boy. At the school, Joseph had been something of a layabout mornings, continually late for breakfast and yawning through the first class of the day.

"Tom needed help," Joseph said solemnly.

Juliana felt a pang, knowing why Joseph was so eager to be useful. He hoped to land a job on Stillwater Springs Ranch, earn enough money to get himself and Theresa home to North Dakota. With luck, the Bureau of Indian Affairs would leave them alone.

"We can always use another hand around here," Lincoln said.

Juliana shot him a glance. "Joseph has school today."

Some of the milk slopped over the edge of the bucket as Joseph set it down hard in the sink. A flush pounded along his fine cheekbones.

"School?" Lincoln asked.

Just then, Gracie burst in, dressed in a light woolen dress and high-button shoes and pulling Daisy behind her by one hand and Billy-Moses by the other. Both children stared at her as though they'd never seen such a wondrous creature, and most likely they hadn't.

"School?" Gracie chirped, her eyes enormous. "Where? When?"

Juliana smiled, rested her hands lightly on her hips. She hadn't bothered to put up her hair; it hung in a long braid over her shoulder. "Here," she said. "At the kitchen table, directly after breakfast."

Joseph groaned.

"Can I learn, too?" Gracie asked breathlessly. "Can I, please?"

"May I," Juliana corrected, ever the teacher. "And I don't see why you shouldn't join us."

"Will you teach me numbers?" Gracie prattled, her words fairly tumbling over one another in her eagerness. "I'm not very good with numbers. I can read, though. And I promise to sit very still and listen to everything you say and raise my hand when I want to speak—"

"Gracie," Lincoln interrupted.

Releasing Daisy and Billy-Moses, Gracie whirled on her father. "Oh, Papa," she blurted, "you're *not* going to say I can't, are you?"

Lincoln's smile was a little wan, and his gaze shifted briefly to Juliana before swinging back to Gracie's upturned face. "No," he said. "I'm not going to say you can't. It's just that Miss Mitchell will be moving on soon and I don't want you to be let down when she does."

The words shouldn't have shaken Juliana—they were quite true, after all, since she *would* be moving on soon, though the means she would employ to do that were still a mystery—but they did. She felt slightly breathless, the way she had the day Clay told her she was no longer welcome in the mansion on Pine Street.

Gracie's eyes brimmed with tears, and Juliana knew they were genuine. She longed to embrace the child, the way she would Daisy or Billy-Moses, if they ever cried. Which, being stoic little creatures, they didn't.

"I just want to *learn things* while I can, Papa," she said.

Tom broke into the conversation, pumping water at the sink. Washing up with a misshapen bar of yellow soap. "I'll get breakfast on the stove," he interjected. His gaze moved to Juliana's face. "We could use Joseph's help today, if you can spare him."

Joseph looked so hopeful that Juliana's throat tightened.

"I'll hear your reading lesson after supper," she relented.

Joseph's grin warmed her like sunshine. "I promise I'll do good," he said.

"Well," Juliana said. "You will do *well,* Joseph, not 'good'."

He nodded, clearly placating her.

When Juliana turned back to Gracie, she saw that the child was leaning against Lincoln's side, sniffling, her arms around his lean waist. The flow of tears had stopped.

"Saint Nicholas is going to bring me a dictionary for Christmas," Gracie announced. She looked up at her father. "Do you think he got my letter, Papa? He won't bring me a doll or anything like that, just because you already *have* a dictionary on your desk and he thinks I could use that instead of having one of my own? Yours is *old*—a lot of words aren't even in it."

Lincoln grinned, tugged lightly at one of Gracie's ringlets. "I'm sure Saint Nick got your letter, sweetheart," he said.

"Who's that?" Theresa asked, trailing into the room, hair unbrushed. Juliana wondered if Lincoln had heard her prayers, as he probably had Gracie's. Told her to sleep well.

"You don't know who Saint Nicholas is?" Gracie asked, astounded.

"We'll discuss him later," Juliana promised, "when we sit down for lessons after breakfast."

"I could recite," Gracie offered. "I know all about Saint Nicholas."

"Gracie," Lincoln said.

"Well, I *do,* Papa. I've read Mr. Moore's poem *dozens* of times."

"We'll have cornmeal mush," Tom decided aloud. "Maybe some sausage."

"What?" Lincoln asked.

"Breakfast," Tom explained with a slight grin. Then he turned to Joseph. "You know how to use a separator, boy?"

Joseph nodded. "We had a milk cow out at the school," he said. "For a while."

Separating the milk from the cream had always been Theresa's chore, since Joseph considered it "woman's work." Mary Rose and Angelique had taken turns churning the butter.

And then the cow had sickened and died, and Mr. Philbert hadn't requisitioned the government for another.

Sadness and frustration swept over Juliana, and it must have shown in her face, because, to her utter surprise, Lincoln laid a hand on her shoulder.

Something startling and fiery raced through her at his

touch. She nearly flinched, and she saw by his expression that he'd noticed.

"Sit down," he said, watching with amusement in his dark eyes as she blushed with an oddly delicious mortification. "I'll get you some coffee."

Chapter Three

The sky was a clear, heart-piercing blue, and sunshine glittered on fields of snow rolling to the base of the foothills and crowning the trees. Creek water shimmered beneath sheets of ice, and the cattle, more than a hundred of them, milled and bawled, impatient for the first load of hay to hit the ground. Lincoln sat in the saddle, his horse restless beneath him, and pulled his hat down over his eyes against the dazzling glare.

He watched as Joseph climbed into the back of the sleigh—the snow was too deep out on the range for a wagon to pass—while Tom soothed the two enormous draft horses hitched to it.

Ben Gainer, a young ranch hand who'd stayed on for the winter because his wife, Rose-of-Sharon, was soon to be delivered of their first child, rode up alongside Lincoln on a spotted pony, a shovel in one hand.

"Best break up some of that ice on the creek," Gainer said.

Lincoln nodded, swung down from the saddle. It was there to be done, as his father used to say. When cattle weren't hungry, they were thirsty, and they weren't smart enough to eat snow or trample the ice with their hooves so they could get to the water beneath. He went to the sleigh, helped himself to one of the pickaxes Tom had brought along.

Wishing, as he sometimes did, that he'd chosen an easier life—Beth's father had offered him a partnership in his Boston law firm—Lincoln went to the creekside and began shattering ice an inch thick, two in some places.

If he'd stayed in Boston, he reflected, Beth might have lived, the two babies, too. Gracie would have been able to go to a real school, too.

Inwardly, Lincoln sighed. Left in Wes's incapable hands,

the ranch would be gone by now, his mother displaced, Tom Dancingstar ripped up by the roots and left to wander in a world that not only underestimated him, but often scorned him, too. All because he was an Indian.

He'd been caught between the devil and the deep blue sea, Lincoln had, and if he'd made the wrong choice, there was no changing it now. The ranch wasn't making him rich, but he'd gotten it back in the black with a lot of hard work and Creed determination.

But what a price he'd paid.

Tom appeared beside him, toting another pickax. Sent Gainer and Joseph back to the hay barn, nearer the house, where the two remaining ranch hands, Art Bentley and Mike Falstaff, waited to load the sleigh up again.

"You look mighty grim this mornin'," Tom observed.

"Hard work," Lincoln said without looking at his friend.

"You've been working since you were nine. I don't think it's that."

Lincoln stopped to catch his breath, sighed. Cattle nosed up behind him, scenting the water. "You going to insist on chatting?" he asked.

Tom chuckled. Cattle pushed past them to get to the creek, so they moved a little farther down the line, out of their way. "Something's thrown you, that's for sure. I reckon it's Miss Juliana Mitchell."

Lincoln felt a surge of touchy exasperation, which was unlike him. He started swinging the pickax again. "I might have had a thought or two where she's concerned," he admitted.

Tom laid a hand on his arm. "She needs a place to light. You need a wife and Gracie needs a mother. Why don't you just offer for Juliana and be done with it?"

A growl of frustration escaped Lincoln. He drove the pickax deep into the hard ice, felt satisfaction as the glaze splintered. "It's not that simple," he said in his own good time.

"Isn't it?" Tom asked.

"I'm paying you to work," Lincoln pointed out, humorless, "not spout advice for the lovelorn."

"Is that what you are?" Tom asked, and looking sidelong, Lincoln saw amusement dancing in the older man's eyes. "Lovelorn?"

"No, damn it," Lincoln snapped.

Tom was relentless. "You're a young man, Lincoln. You ought to have a woman. Gracie ought to have a mother, brothers and sisters. If you were willing to bring in a stranger from someplace else and put a wedding band on her finger, why not Juliana?"

"I was hoping for a governess or a housekeeper," Lincoln said. "Taking a wife was a last resort."

"All right, then," Tom persisted, "Juliana's a teacher. She would make a fine governess. Maybe even a decent housekeeper."

"She won't want to stay out here on this ranch," Lincoln argued. "She's a city girl—you can see that by the way she moves, hear it in the way she talks."

"Beth was a city girl, and she liked the ranch fine."

It was all Lincoln could do not to fling the pickax so far and so hard that it would lodge in the snow on the other side of the creek. Tom sometimes went days without talking at all; now, all of a sudden, he was running off at the mouth like a lonely spinster at high tea. "Why? Why is this different, Lincoln? Because you think you could care about Juliana?"

Lincoln didn't answer because he couldn't. His throat felt raw, and a cow bumped him from behind, nearly sent him sprawling into the cold creek water. "I loved Beth," he said after a long time, because Tom would have kept at him until he gave some kind of answer.

Tom laid a hand on his shoulder. "I know that," he said. "But Beth is gone, and you're still here. You and Gracie. That child is lonesome, Lincoln—sometimes it hurts my heart just to look at her. And you're not doing much better."

"I'm doing fine. And there are worse things than being lonesome."

"Are there? You going to tell me you don't lie in there in that bed at night and wish there was a woman beside you?"

Again, Lincoln couldn't answer.

Mercifully, the talk-fest seemed to be over. Tom went back to work, another load of hay arrived, Joseph and young Gainer threw it to the cattle and went back for more.

Toward noon, satisfied that the stock would neither starve nor perish of thirst, Lincoln sent the whole crew back to have their midday meal in the bunkhouse kitchen and then tend to other chores around the place, like splitting firewood and mending harnesses and mucking out stalls in the barn. Winter work could be miserably hard, but the season had its favorable side. There was a lot of time for catching up on lost sleep and sitting around a potbellied stove, swapping yarns.

Gainer, Lincoln knew, was always anxious about his

wife, fearing she'd run into some kind of baby trouble, alone in the tiny cabin they shared, and he wouldn't be there to help.

God knew, the possibility was real enough. Beth might have bled to death with the first miscarriage if Cora hadn't been around. She'd gone out onto the back porch, Lincoln's mother had, and clanged at the iron triangle with vigor until they'd heard the signal, out on the range, and ridden for home.

What if Beth had been alone with Gracie, who was only two at the time?

Lincoln stuck a foot into the stirrup and swung up onto his horse's back. No sense in agonizing over something that was over and done with. He'd raced to town for the doctor, but it had been Tom Dancingstar who'd stopped Beth's bleeding. By the time Lincoln returned with help, Cora had bathed and bundled the lifeless baby, a boy.

Lincoln had sat in the rocking chair in the kitchen, holding his son, and wept without shame until sunset when he'd carried him out to the graveyard beyond the orchard, dug a tiny grave and laid the child to rest. Eighteen months later, Beth had given birth to a second daughter, stillborn.

He'd wept then, too, though not in front of his distraught wife. That time, Tom and Wes had done the burying, and more than a month had gone by before the circuit preacher stopped by to say prayers over the grave.

Turning his horse homeward, Lincoln set the memories aside, but they seemed to trail along in his wake like ghosts. Clouds gathered, black-gray in the eastern sky, bulging with snow.

Feeding the cattle would be harder tomorrow, cold work that would sting his hands, even inside heavy leather gloves, but mostly likely the creek wouldn't freeze again.

His heart seemed to travel on ahead of him, drawn to the light and warmth of the house. Drawn to Juliana.

Reaching the barn, he unsaddled his horse, rubbed the animal down with a wad of burlap and gave him a scoop of grain in the bottom of a wooden bucket. He was putting off going into the house, not because he didn't want to, though. No, he was savoring the prospect.

The first snowflakes began to fall, slow and fat, as he left the barn, and the sun was veiled, bringing on a premature twilight.

Lanterns shone in the kitchen windows, and Lincoln

raised the collar of his coat, ducked his head against the wind and quickened his stride.

Gracie met him at the back door, her face as bright as any lantern, her eyes huge. "I'm learning the multiplication tables!" she fairly shouted. "And I gave a recitation about Saint Nicholas, too!"

Lincoln smiled, bent to kiss the top of Gracie's head, then eased her backward into the kitchen, out of the cold. The table was clear of the slates and books that had come out of Juliana's satchel that morning after breakfast was over, and she was at the stove, stirring last night's venison stew.

She turned her head, favored him with a shy smile, and it struck him that she was not just womanly, but beautiful. She made that faded calico dress of hers look like the finest velvet, and he wanted to touch her fiery hair.

Instead, he hung his hat on its peg, shrugged out of his coat and hung that, too. "School over for the day?"

She nodded. "We accomplished a lot," she said quietly.

Lincoln smiled down at Gracie again. "So I hear," he replied. "Where are the others?"

"Theresa's putting Daisy and Billy-Moses down for their naps," Juliana answered, seeming pleased that he'd asked. "Joseph is with Tom—they spotted a flock of wild turkeys and they're hoping to bring back a big one for Christmas dinner."

Christmas. He'd forgotten all about that, and it was coming up fast. Fortunately, he'd already bought Gracie's dictionary, and his mother had taken care of the rest. There was a stash of peppermint sticks, books, doll clothes and other gifts hidden away on the high shelf of Cora's wardrobe; she'd shown him the loot before she left on her trip, and admonished him not to forget to put up a tree.

As though reading his mind, Gracie tugged at his sleeve. "Are we getting a Christmas tree?"

Lincoln thought it was a foolish thing to cut down a living tree, minding its own business in some copse or forest, and he flat-out refused to allow any lighted candles in the branches. But he always gave in and hiked out into the woods with an ax, and nailed two chunks of wood crisscross for a stand, because it meant so much to his little girl. "Don't we always?" he countered.

"I thought you might change your mind this year," Gracie said. "You said it was a very *German* thing to do. What's German?"

It was Juliana, the schoolmarm, who answered.

"Germany is a country, like the United States and Canada. People from Germany are…?"

"Germans!" Gracie cried in triumph.

"Very good," Juliana said, with pleasure growing in her eyes.

"Go take a nap," Lincoln told his daughter.

"Papa, I never take naps," Gracie reminded him. "I'm not a *baby.*"

"Neither are Daisy and Billy-Moses," Lincoln said. "Go."

Gracie turned to Juliana. "Is *Theresa* going to take a nap?"

At that moment, Theresa entered the kitchen, and it was apparent, by the sparkle of collusion in her eyes, that she'd heard at least part of the exchange. She held out a hand to Gracie. "Come," she said. "We'll just lie down for a while and rest. We don't have to sleep, and I'll read you a story."

"I'll read *you* a story," Gracie insisted.

Theresa smiled, nodded slightly.

Gracie could never resist any opportunity to show off her uncanny mastery of the written word. When she was barely three years old, Beth had taught her the alphabet, and after that, she'd been able to divine the mechanics of the reading process. It was as if the child had been *born* knowing how to make sense of books.

Lincoln felt a pang, thinking of Beth when he wanted so badly to be alone in that kitchen with Juliana, for whatever time Providence might allot them. It wasn't as if he meant to touch her, or "offer for her," the way Tom had suggested out there by the creek. She warmed him deep down, that was all. In places where the heat from the cookstove didn't reach.

When Gracie and Theresa were gone, though, he just stood there, mute as a stump.

"Wash up," Juliana told him, keeping her gaze averted. "You must be hungry."

He went to the sink, rolled up his sleeves, pumped some water and lathered his hands with soap. It was harsh stuff, fit to take the hide off, as his mother complained.

Juliana fetched a bowl and spoon, dished up stew for him. The task was ordinary enough, but it made Lincoln think about the conversation with Tom again.

He drew back his chair at the table, sat down. "Did you eat?" he asked, because he wanted Juliana to join him.

She nodded. "Coffee?"

"You don't have to wait on me, Juliana," he replied.

"Nonsense," she replied, bustling off, returning to the table with a steaming mug. "You've given us food and shelter, and I want to show my gratitude." A twinkle sparked in her eyes. "But I draw the line at polishing your boots, Mr. Creed."

"I guess you wouldn't be looking for a housekeeper's job," Lincoln said, and then wished he could bite off his tongue. Juliana Mitchell might have fallen on hard times, but she wasn't cut out to be a servant, even if she *had* poured him coffee and heated up last night's stew for lunch.

She sat down, though, and that was encouraging.

"Are you offering?" she asked, almost shyly.

Lincoln went still, his spoon midway between the bowl and his mouth. "Would you accept if I did?"

Juliana shifted in her chair. Folded her hands in her lap. "My brother would probably come here and drag me back to Denver by the hair if I did," she said, and she sounded almost rueful.

"Your brother?" *Yes, fool,* taunted an impatient voice in his head. *You know what a brother is. You have two of them yourself, three if you count poor Dawson, lying out there in the cemetery next to your pa.*

A fetching blush played on her cheekbones. Lincoln tried to imagine her scrubbing floors, beating rugs, ironing shirts and emptying chamber pots, and found it impossible. For all that her dress had seen better days, there was something innately aristocratic about this woman, something finely honed in the way she held herself, even sitting in a chair.

"Clay had enough trouble reconciling himself to my being a teacher," Juliana said after a few awkward moments during which she swallowed a lot. "So far he's left me alone, but he'd have a fit if I took to keeping house. Unless I was married—"

Her voice fell away, and the blush intensified. Now, Lincoln suspected, *she* was the one wanting to bite off her tongue.

"What if you were a governess?" he ventured, lowering the spoon back to his bowl even though he felt half-starved.

She shrugged both shoulders and looked miserable. "I suppose he'd see that as an improvement over teaching in an Indian School," she allowed.

Lincoln wanted to close his hand over hers and squeeze some comfort into her, but he didn't. "You do everything your brother tells you?" he asked, surprised.

"No," she said, meeting his eyes at last, trying to smile.

He'd intended no criticism by his question, and to his great relief, she seemed to know that. "If that were so, I'd be a wealthy widow now, living in Denver."

Lincoln raised one eyebrow, waited.

She did some more blushing. "Clay wanted me to marry his business partner. I'd resigned myself to that, even though I was going to Normal School. But then my grandmother died and I'd graduated, and I realized I wanted to *use* what I'd learned."

There was more she wasn't saying, Lincoln knew that, but he didn't push. The situation seemed too fragile for that. Slowly, to give her a chance to recover a little, he looked down at his bowl, stuck his spoon into the stew and began to eat.

"This Clay yahoo wouldn't like your being a governess?" he asked carefully, when some time had passed.

She laughed softly, probably at the term *yahoo* applied to her no-doubt powerful brother. "Probably not."

"Why? Because he'd think it was beneath you?" Again, there was no scorn in the inquiry.

"No," Juliana said, with quiet bitterness. "He'd think it was beneath *him,* and he's already despairing of my reputation. To Clay, my teaching other people's children—

especially *Indian* children—is tantamount to serving drinks in a saloon."

Again, Lincoln waited. Some process was unfolding, and it had to be let alone.

"It's starting to snow," Juliana said wistfully, her gaze turned to the window again.

"What will you do, then?" Lincoln asked. "After you leave here, I mean?"

She sighed. Met his gaze. "I don't know," she confessed.

"I guess we could get married," Lincoln said.

Juliana opened her mouth, closed it again.

Lincoln felt crimson heat climbing his neck, pulsing along the underside of his jawline. "You heard Fred Willand say it in the mercantile yesterday," he said, his voice raspy. "I've been advertising for a housekeeper or a governess, or both, for better than a year. Failing that, I'd settle for a wife."

Juliana began to laugh. Her eyes glistened with unshed tears, and she put a hand to her mouth to silence herself.

"I didn't mean 'settle,' exactly—"

"Yes, you did," Juliana said. Her look softened. "You loved Gracie's mother a lot, didn't you?"

"Yes," Lincoln answered readily.

"So much that you can't make room in your heart for another woman," Juliana speculated. "That's why you'd marry a stranger, someone answering a newspaper advertisement. Because you wouldn't have to care for that person."

She wasn't accusing him of anything; he knew that by her tone and her bearing. Most likely, the words stung the way they did because they were only too true.

"And that person wouldn't have to care for me," he replied.

"But you'd expect her to—to share your bed?"

"Sooner or later, yes," Lincoln said. "That's part of being a wife, isn't it?"

Juliana propped an elbow on the table, cupped her chin in her palm. They might have been discussing hog prices, she was so unruffled and matter-of-fact. "I suppose," she agreed.

Before things could go any further, Tom and Joseph banged in through the back door, their faces white-slashed with broad smiles.

"Christmas dinner's outside," Tom said. Then his glance traveled between Juliana and Lincoln, and he sobered a little.

Joseph, being so young, and buoyed by the pride of accomplishment, didn't notice that they'd interrupted something, he and Tom. "We got two turkeys," he announced proudly. "Tom's already gutted them, but we have to pluck them yet, and I might have to pick some buckshot out of the one I got."

Juliana winced.

Lincoln smiled. Pushed back his chair and stood, carrying his bowl and spoon to the sink.

"Better have some stew," he told Tom and the boy.

"And then I'll hear you read today's lesson," Juliana told Joseph.

The boy's face fell briefly, then he smiled again. A deal, he must have decided, was a deal. Juliana had allowed him to skip his schoolwork earlier so he could work with the men out on the range. Now she wanted her due.

"After I pluck the turkeys?"

"After you pluck the turkeys," Juliana conceded with a fond sigh. "And you're not bringing those poor dead creatures into the house to do it."

The command was downright wifely, and that pleased Lincoln, though he didn't let it show. The idea had taken root in his mind, and in Juliana's, too, and for now, that was enough.

Joseph's grin faltered a little. "Remember last Christmas, Miss Mitchell, when you tried to roast that turkey that farmer's wife gave us and it smoked so much that we had to open the doors and all the windows?"

"Thank you, Joseph," Juliana said mildly, "for that reminder."

Tom smiled at that.

Lincoln glanced at the windows, saw that the snow was coming down harder and faster. Through the flurries, he glimpsed his brother Wes riding up, leading a pack mule behind him, a huge pine tree bound to its back.

"I'll be damned," he muttered with a low, throaty chuckle, and headed for the back door, pausing just long enough to put on his coat.

Wes wore no hat, and snowflakes gathered in his dark chestnut hair and fringed his eyelashes. His grin was as white as the snowy ground, and even from ten feet away, Lincoln could smell the whiskey and cigar smoke on him.

"Ma said she'd have my hide if I didn't make sure Gracie had a Christmas tree," Wes said cheerfully. "So here I am."

Lincoln laughed and shook his head. "Did you happen to credit that there's another blizzard coming on and it'll be pitch-dark by the time you get back to town?"

"I've got enough whiskey in me to prevent any possibility of freezing," Wes answered. He took a cheroot from the pocket of his scruffy coat, fitted at the waist like something a dandified gambler would wear, and clamped it between his perfect teeth. "Fact is, I might need a swallow or two before I head home, just the same."

Dismounting, Wes went back to the mule and began untying the ropes that secured the Christmas tree to the animal. The lush, piney fragrance his motions stirred reminded Lincoln of their boyhood. They hadn't been raised to believe in Saint Nicholas, but there had always been fresh green boughs all over the house, and modest presents waiting at their places at the breakfast table on Christmas morning.

"Are you just going to stand there," Wes grumped, grinning all the while, "or will you lend me a hand getting this tree into the house?"

"It's too wet to be in the house," Lincoln said, sounding a mite wifely himself. "We'll set it in the woodshed, let it dry off a little."

"Whatever you say, little brother," Wes replied affably, even though he was six inches shorter than Lincoln and only two years older. "Fred Willand told me when I stopped off at the mercantile to see if you'd gotten any mail—you didn't—that you've got a woman out here. That pretty teacher from the Indian School."

Lincoln took hold of the sizable tree. It was a wonder the weight of the thing hadn't buckled that poor old mule's knees—he'd have to saw a good foot off the thing to stand it up in the front room. "Fred Willand," he said, through the boughs, "gossips like an old woman."

Wes laughed at that. "Hell," he said, "if it weren't for Fred, I wouldn't know what you were up to half the time. It's not as if you ever stop by the saloon or the newspaper office to flap your jaws."

"I don't have much time for flapping my jaws," Lincoln answered. In spite of nearly losing the ranch because of Wes's well-intentioned mismanagement, he'd always loved his brother. After Dawson's death, the old man had taken his grief out on his second son, since Micah, being the eldest, would have given as good as he got. Lincoln, taking Dawson's place as the youngest in the family, had stayed clear of his pa and taken to following Tom Dancingstar everywhere he went.

Wes looked up, his eyes serious now. "Ma's gone," he said. "I can feel the peace even from out here."

Their mother didn't approve of Wes's drinking, his poker playing and cigar smoking, or the woman he loved, and she made that clear every time she got the opportunity. So Wes stayed away from the ranch house when she was around.

Lincoln started for the woodshed, dragging the massive tree behind him. "Go on inside and have some of Tom's venison stew," he called over one shoulder. "It's probably been a month since you've had a decent meal."

"I wouldn't miss a chance to drag my eyeballs over a good-looking woman," Wes responded.

Lincoln didn't dignify that with an answer, but it made him grin to himself just the same.

When he came out of the woodshed, he saw that Wes had left the horse and mule standing. Lincoln led them both into the barn, out of the icy wind, unsaddled the horse, fed and watered both creatures, and rubbed them down the way he'd done with his own mount earlier.

He'd been doing things his brother should have done for as long as he could remember, but he didn't mind, because Wes was always the one who showed up at the most unlikely times with the most unlikely gifts.

ALTHOUGH JULIANA PUT ON A GOOD show, she was shaken inside, and it wasn't just because Lincoln Creed had all but proposed marriage to her at his kitchen table a little while before. She might actually say yes, if he did, and that jarred her to the quick.

John Holden would have made a perfectly acceptable husband, despite his obnoxious daughters, but she'd refused him. Other men had tried to court her during the intervening years, too, though she'd discouraged them, as well. She'd always imagined that if she ever married, it would happen in a fit of wild, romantic passion. She'd be swept off her feet, overcome with desire.

Lincoln stirred something in her, something almost primal—that was undeniable. But wild, romantic passion? No.

On the other hand, she knew he was kind, generous. That he worked hard, was an attentive father and didn't judge people by the culture they'd been born into. That he let his suspenders loop at his sides in the mornings while he shaved.

She smiled at the image, even as Tom introduced her to Weston Creed, and Gracie ran shrieking for joy into the kitchen, hurling herself into her laughing uncle's arms.

He swung her around. "Brought you a Christmas tree," he told her. "Your papa is putting it in the woodshed to dry off a little. What's Saint Nicholas going to bring you this year?"

Gracie paused at the question and her lower lip trembled. A troubled expression flickered across her perfect face.

"I hope he doesn't come," she confided, in a whisper that carried.

Weston looked genuinely puzzled, though Juliana suspected everything he said and did was exaggerated. "Why would you hope for a thing like that?"

"Because he doesn't know the others are here," she said, near tears. "And I don't want any presents if Billy-Moses and Daisy and Joseph and Theresa don't get some, too."

Juliana's heart melted and slid down the inside of her rib cage. If Lincoln *did* propose, she might just accept. She wasn't in love with him—but she adored his daughter.

Chapter Four

When Lincoln got back inside the house, he found Wes standing in the middle of the kitchen, holding a dismayed Gracie in his arms.

"Well," Wes told his niece solemnly, "we'd better get word to Saint Nicholas right quick, then."

Shedding his coat, Lincoln raised an eyebrow.

"Christmas is only four days away," Gracie fretted. "And the train won't come through Stillwater Springs again until *next* week. So how can I write to him in time?"

Lincoln and Juliana exchanged looks: Lincoln's curious, Juliana's wistful.

"Papa," Gracie all but wailed, "could we send a telegraph to Saint Nicholas?"

"What?" Lincoln asked, mystified.

"He won't bring anything for the others, because he doesn't know they're here!" Gracie despaired.

Something shifted deep in Lincoln's heart, and it wasn't just because he was standing so close to Juliana that their shoulders nearly touched. When had he moved?

He thought of the gifts on the shelf in his mother's wardrobe, the box of watercolor paints he'd bought on impulse back at the mercantile the day before. "Oh, I already did that," he lied easily.

Gracie was not only generous, she was formidably bright. Her forehead creased as Wes set her gently on her feet. "When?" she asked skeptically.

"In town yesterday," Lincoln said. "Soon as I knew we were going to have company, I went straight to the telegraph office and sent the old fella a wire."

Gracie's eyes widened, while her busy mind weighed the logistics. Fortunately, she came down on the side of relief rather than reason, and Lincoln felt mildly guilty for deceiving her, pure motives or none.

She beamed. "Well," she said. "That's fine, then."

"'Course, he'll probably have to spread things a little thinner than usual," Lincoln added. "Saint Nicholas, I mean. Times are hard, remember."

Gracie was undaunted. "All I want is a dictionary," she said. "So I can learn all the words there are in the whole world."

Lincoln wanted to sweep her up into his arms, the way Wes had apparently done upon arrival, but he figured that would be laying things on a little thick, so he just replied quietly, "I'm proud of you, Gracie Creed."

Beside him, Juliana sniffled once, but when he looked, he saw that she was smiling. Her eyes glistened a little, though.

Seeing he was watching her, Juliana turned quickly and busied herself scraping the last of the stew from the kettle into a bowl and basically herding a clearly charmed Wes over to the table.

She didn't even make him wash up, which might have galled Lincoln a little, if he hadn't been so busy thinking what a fine daughter he and Beth had brought into the world.

Although Wes loved his woman, Kate, and to Lincoln's knowledge his brother hadn't been unfaithful from the day the two of them had taken up with each other, his amber-colored eyes trailed Juliana's every movement, danced with mischief whenever he met Lincoln's gaze.

He *knew,* damn it. Wes knew Juliana had his younger brother's insides in a tangle, and he was bound to rib him without mercy.

"You'd better spend the night," Lincoln said to his brother, even though, at the moment, that was about the last thing he wanted. "Snow's coming down hard."

Wes shook his head, shifted slightly so Gracie could plant herself on his knee. "I've gotta get back. Poker game."

It wasn't long before he'd finished his meal and said goodbye to Gracie. This, too, was like Wes—he'd been uncomfortable in the house since Dawson died. Once, he'd even confided privately that he half expected their murdered brother to tap him on the shoulder from behind.

Gracie went off in search of the other children, and Tom and Joseph were still outside plucking turkeys. Avoiding Juliana's eyes, just as he sensed she was avoiding his, Lincoln put his coat on again, followed Wes into the cold and walked alongside him toward the barn.

About midway, Wes chuckled and shook his head, then gave a low whistle. He hadn't even hesitated when his horse and mule weren't where he'd left them; he knew Lincoln would have attended to anything he'd left undone.

"What?" Lincoln asked, sounding peevish because he knew what the answer would be.

"You," Wes said happily, snow gathering on his hair and shoulders and eyelashes again. "Every time you looked at that schoolmarm, I thought I was going to have to roll your tongue up like a rug and shove it back in your mouth."

Lincoln felt his neck warm. He was half again too stubborn to honor Wes's good-natured taunt with a reply of any kind.

Wes laughed outright then, and slapped Lincoln hard on the back as they slogged heavily through the snow. "She's smitten with you, little brother," he went on. "I figured I'd better tell you that, since you can be a mite thickheaded when it comes to women."

"I suppose *you're* an expert?" Lincoln bit out, raising his collar again. Damn, it was colder than a well-digger's ass. If he could have willed green grass to sprout up right through the snow, he would have done it.

Wes laughed again. "If you don't believe me, just ask Kate," he said lightly.

Lincoln happened to like Kate, even if she was a "light-skirt," as his old-fashioned mother put it, but he wasn't about to put any questions to her, especially when it came to something that personal.

He was silent until they entered the barn, now nearly dark. Both of them knew every inch of the place, and neither of them hesitated to let their eyes adjust to the lack of light.

"Thanks," Lincoln said awkwardly. "For the tree, I mean."

Wes found his horse and opened the stall door, began saddling up. "That was for Gracie," he said. "You want me to stop by Willand's Mercantile and get some presents for those other kids?"

The offer touched Lincoln. "No," he said, his voice sounding gruff. "Ma laid in a good supply of stuff before she left. There'll be plenty to go around."

Wes nodded. "That's good," he said.

"I guess you must have seen Ma recently?" Lincoln ventured. Their mother was a sore spot between them; Lincoln accepted that she was a little on the irritating side, while Wes still seemed to think she ought to change anytime now. "I dropped her off at the depot myself, and there was no sign of you."

There was no humor in Wes's chuckle this time. "She sent Fred Willand's boy, Charlie, around to the newspaper office with a note. 'Course, I'd have lit a cigar with it if it hadn't been for Gracie."

Lincoln frowned. Just as their mother wasn't fixing to change, Wes wasn't, either. Both of them were waiting for the other to see the error of their ways and repent like a convert at a tent meeting, and that would happen on the proverbial cold day in hell. "You think it's wrong, letting Gracie believe in this Saint Nicholas fella?"

Wes lowered the stirrup, gave the saddle a yank to make sure it was secure, then swung up. "She's a child," he said. Lincoln couldn't make out his features in the shadows. "Children need to believe in things while they can. I'll leave the mule here for a day or two, if it's all the same to you."

Lincoln nodded, stepped forward, hoping in vain for a better look at his brother's face, and took hold of the reins to stop Wes from riding out. "Do you believe in anything, Wes?" he asked, struck by how much the answer mattered to him.

Wes sighed. "I believe in Kate. I believe in five-card

stud and whiskey and the sacred qualities of a good cigar. I believe in Gracie and—damn it, I must be sobering up—I believe in your good judgment, little brother. Use it. Don't let that schoolmarm get away."

"I've only known her since yesterday," Lincoln reasoned. He was always the one inclined to reason. Wes just did whatever seemed like a good idea at the time.

"Maybe that's long enough," Wes answered.

Lincoln let go of the reins.

Wes executed a jaunty salute, there in the shadows, and rode toward the door of the barn, ducking his head as he passed under it.

"Rub that horse down when you get back to town," Lincoln called after his brother. "Don't just leave him standing at the hitching post in front of the saloon."

Wes didn't answer; maybe he hadn't heard.

More likely, he'd heard fine. He just hadn't felt called upon to bother with a reply.

THE TURKEY CARCASSES HAD BEEN trussed with twine and tied to a high branch in a tree so they'd stay cold and the wolves and coyotes wouldn't get them. Looking out the window as she stood at the sink, Juliana watched the pale forms sway in the thickening snow and the purple gathering of twilight.

She was certain she would never be hungry again.

Behind her, seated at the table, Tom Dancingstar puffed on a corncob pipe, making the air redolent with cherry-scented tobacco, while Joseph droned laboriously through the assigned three pages of a Charles Dickens novel. The other children had gathered in the front room near the fireplace; the last time Juliana had looked in on them, Theresa and Gracie were playing checkers, while Daisy examined one of Gracie's dolls and Billy-Moses stacked wooden alphabet blocks, knocked them over and stacked them again.

The afternoon had dragged on, and Juliana wondered when Lincoln would come back into the house, when they'd get a chance to talk alone again, whether or not she ought to attempt to start supper.

It wasn't that she didn't *want* to cook. She hadn't been allowed near the kitchen as a young girl—Cook hadn't wanted a child underfoot—and every school she'd taught at until Stillwater Springs had provided meals in a common dining room.

Now, resurrected by Joseph's account, the image of last

Christmas's burned turkey rose in her mind. They'd managed to save some of it and eaten around the charred parts. After that, probably tired of oatmeal and boiled beans, the construction of which Juliana had been able to discern by pouring over an old cookery book, Theresa and Mary Rose had taken to preparing most of the meals.

A snapping sound made Juliana jump, turn quickly.

Joseph had closed the Dickens novel smartly. "Finished," he said. "Can— *May* I go out and help Tom with the chores?"

Juliana blinked. A fine teacher *she* was—for all she knew, Joseph might have been reading from the back of a medicine bottle instead of a book. She had no idea whether he'd stumbled over any of the words, or lost track of the flow of the narrative and had to begin again, the way he often did.

So she bluffed.

"Tell me what happened in the story," she said.

Joseph was ready. "This woman named Nancy got herself beat to death by that Bill Sykes fella."

He'd been reading from *Oliver Twist,* then.

"He was a bad'un," Tom remarked seriously. "That Sykes, I mean."

"He was indeed," Juliana agreed. "You may help with the chores, Joseph."

Tom sighed, rose to his feet. "You reckon you could start that story over from the first, next time you read?" he asked the boy. "I'd like to know what led up to a poor girl winding up in such a fix."

Joseph would have balked at the request had it come from Juliana. Since it came from Tom instead, he beamed and said, "Sure."

"When?" Tom asked, starting for the back door, bent on getting the chores done, his pipe caught between his teeth.

"Maybe after supper," Joseph answered.

Supper. Renewed anxiety rushed through Juliana.

And Tom gave his trademark chuckle. The man probably couldn't read, at least not well enough to tackle Dickens, but he soon proved he *could* read minds.

"I'll fry up some eggs when we're through in the barn," he told Juliana. "And Mrs. Creed put up some bear-meat preserves last fall—mighty good, mixed in with fried potatoes."

Bear-meat preserves? That sounded about as appetizing to Juliana as the naked turkeys dangling from the tree branch outside, but she managed not to make a face.

"You have enough to do," she said, with a bright confidence she most certainly didn't feel. "I can fry eggs."

"No, you can't," Joseph argued benignly. "Remember when…?"

"Joseph."

The boy shrugged both shoulders, and he and Tom let in a rush of cold air opening the door to go out.

The instant they were gone, Juliana hurried to the front room and beckoned to Theresa with a crooked finger.

Theresa obediently left her checker game and Gracie to approach.

"Quick," Juliana whispered, fraught with a strange urgency. "Come and show me how to fry eggs!"

WHEN LINCOLN CAME IN WITH an armload of firewood, he found Juliana and Theresa side by side in front of the stove, working away, and the kitchen smelled of savory things—eggs, potatoes frying in onions, some kind of meat. Gracie was busy setting the table.

His stomach grumbled. The venison stew had worn off a while ago.

"Where have you been, Papa?" Gracie asked, all but singing the words, and dancing to them, too. "Did you ride all the way to town with Uncle Wes so he wouldn't get lost in the snow?"

Lincoln smiled and shook his head no. "Wes's horse knows the way home, even if your uncle doesn't," he said. Actually, he'd been in the Gainers' cabin, admiring the spindly little Christmas tree Ben had put up for his child-heavy wife and drinking weak coffee. And at once avoiding and anticipating his return to the house, to Juliana.

Gracie nodded sagely. "That's a good horse," she said.

Lincoln proceeded through the kitchen, then the front room, and along the hallway to Juliana's door. Tonight, he thought, entering with the wood and kindling, he wouldn't have to lie awake worrying that she and the little boy and girl were cold.

Oh, he'd probably lie awake, all right, but there would be something else on his mind.

He'd made a damn fool of himself, with all that talk about governesses and housekeepers and—he gulped at the recollection—taking a wife.

Unburdening himself of the wood, Lincoln bent to open the stove door. Methodically, he took up the short-handled broom and bucket reserved for the purpose and swept out the ashes. When that was done, he crouched, crumpling newspaper and arranging kindling. In an hour or so, the cold room would be comfortably warm.

"Lincoln?"

Startled, Lincoln turned his head, saw Juliana standing in the doorway, looking like a redheaded angel hiding wings under a threadbare dress. His heart shinnied up into the back of his throat and thumped there.

"Supper's ready," she said.

Another wifely statement. He liked the sound of it. Smiled as he shut the stove door and rose to his full height to adjust the damper on the metal chimney. "Thanks," he said.

She lingered on the threshold, neither in nor out.

Lincoln enjoyed thinking how scandalized his mother would have been if she'd known. Straitlaced, she'd have had a hissy fit at the idea of the two of them standing within spitting distance of a bed—especially when that bed was her own. "Was there something else?"

Juliana swallowed, looked away, visibly forced herself to meet his gaze again. "About the presents—the children would understand. They aren't used to a fuss being made over Christmas, anyway, and—"

Lincoln smiled and went to his mother's massive

wardrobe, opened the door. Gestured for Juliana to come to his side.

Reluctantly, she did so.

He pointed to the top shelf. Games. Dolls. Books. A set of jacks. A fancy comb-and-brush set. Enough candy to rot the teeth of every child in the state of Montana, twice over.

Seeing it all, Juliana widened her eyes.

"There's plenty," he said. "My brother Micah lives a long way from here, in Colorado, so Ma never sees his boys. Wes never married, and as far as we know, he's never fathered a child. That leaves Gracie, and Ma's been bent on spoiling her from the first."

Juliana stepped back, watched as Lincoln closed the wardrobe doors again. "You don't approve?"

"Of what?"

She went pink again. Fetchingly so. "Your mother, buying so many gifts for Gracie."

Lincoln considered, shook his head. "No," he said. "I guess I don't. But it doesn't seem to be hurting her any—Gracie, I mean—and anyhow, my mother is a force to be reckoned with. Most of the time, it's easier to just let her have her way."

Juliana moved closer to the stove, though whether the

objective was to get warm or put some distance between the two of them, Lincoln didn't know. What she said next sideswiped him.

"The Bureau of Indian Affairs is probably going to put me in jail."

Lincoln's breath went shallow. "Why?"

"I was supposed to send these children to Missoula for placement in another school," Juliana said. "Joseph and Theresa have a family, a home, people who want them. Daisy and Billy-Moses will either be swept under some rug or placed in an orphanage. I couldn't bear it."

Lincoln went to her then, took a gentle hold on her shoulders. Tried to ignore the physical repercussions of touching her. "I'll pay the train fare to send Joseph and Theresa home," he said. "But how do you know the bureau won't just drag them out again?"

Gratitude registered in her face, and a degree of relief. "They won't bother," she said with sad confidence. "It would take too long and cost too much."

"The two little ones—they don't have anyone?"

"Just me," Juliana said. "I shouldn't have gotten attached to them—I was warned about that when I first started teaching—but I couldn't help it."

A solution occurred to Lincoln—after all, he was a lawyer—but even in the face of Juliana's despair, talking about it would be premature. His right hand rose of its own accord from her shoulder to her cheek. She did not resist his caress.

"After Christmas," he said, very quietly, "we'll find a way to straighten this out. In the meantime, we've got two turkeys, a tree—" he indicated the wardrobe with a motion of his head "—and enough presents to do Saint Nicholas proud. For now, set the rest aside."

She gazed up at him. "You are a remarkable man, Lincoln Creed. A remarkable man with a remarkable daughter."

Embarrassed pleasure suffused Lincoln. "I think we'd better go and have supper."

Juliana smiled. "I think we'd better," she agreed.

SUPPER WAS A BOISTEROUS AFFAIR with so many people gathered around the table, their faces bathed in lantern light and shadow. And to Juliana's surprise—she forced herself to try some, in order to set a good example for the children—the bear meat turned out to be delicious.

Tom and Joseph did the dishes, while Gracie sat in a

rocking chair nearby, feet dangling high above the floor, reading competently from *Oliver Twist*.

Juliana, banking the fire in the cookstove for the night, stole a glance at Tom and noted that he was listening with close and solemn interest.

Gracie finally read herself to sleep—Billy-Moses and Daisy had long since succumbed, and Lincoln had carried them to bed, one in each arm—and Tom seemed so letdown that Joseph took the book gently from the little girl's hand and picked up where she'd left off.

Juliana hoisted Gracie out of the chair and felt a warm ache in her heart when the child's head came to rest on her shoulder.

She met Lincoln in the corridor leading to the bedrooms. She thought he might take Gracie from her, but he stepped aside instead, his face softening, and watched in silence as she carried his daughter to her bed. A lamp glowed on the nightstand, and Theresa, a pillow propped behind her, was reading one of Gracie's many books.

Juliana set Gracie on her feet, helped her out of her dress and into her nightgown.

Gracie, half awake and half asleep, murmured something and closed her eyes as Juliana tucked her in, kissed her forehead, and then Theresa's.

She took the book from Theresa's hands with a smile, and extinguished the lamp, aware all the while of Lincoln standing in the doorway, watching.

He stepped back again, to let her go by, and smiled when she shivered in the draft and hugged herself.

"I want to show you something," he said.

Curious, she allowed him to lead her to the end of the hallway, where he opened a door, stepped inside and lit a lamp, causing soft light to spill out at Juliana's feet. She hesitated, then followed, and drew in a breath when she saw a porcelain bathtub with a boiler above it, exuding the heat and scent of a wood fire.

Juliana hadn't enjoyed such a luxury since she'd left her grandmother's mansion in Denver. There, she'd taken gaslights and abundant hot water for granted. Since then, she'd survived on sponge baths and the occasional furtive dunk in a washtub.

"I mean to put in a commode and a sink come spring," Lincoln said, sounding shy. "They say we'll have electricity in Stillwater Springs in a few years."

Juliana was nearly overcome. She put a hand to her heart and rested one shoulder against the door frame.

He moved past her, their bodies brushing in the narrow doorway.

Heat pulsed at Juliana's core.

Without another word, Lincoln Creed left her to turn the spigots, find a towel and fetch her nightgown and wrapper from the toasty bedroom, where Daisy and Billy-Moses were already deeply asleep.

The bath was a wonder. A gift. Juliana sank into it, closed her eyes and marveled. When the water finally cooled, she climbed out, dried herself off and donned her nightclothes. A bar of light shone under the door to the room she supposed was Lincoln's, and if it wouldn't have been so brazen, she would have knocked lightly at that door, opened it far enough to say a quiet "Thank you."

Instead, she made her way back to the kitchen, walking softly.

Joseph was still reading from *Oliver Twist,* seated at the table now, and Tom was still listening, smoking his pipe and gazing into space as though seeing the story unfold before his eyes.

Without making a sound, Juliana retreated, smiling to herself.

That night, she slept soundly.

THE SNOW HAD STOPPED BY DAWN, but it reached Lincoln's knees as he made his way toward the barn. Even the draft horses would have a hard time getting through the stuff, but the cattle had to be fed, and that meant hitching up the sled and loading it with hay.

Lincoln thought of Wes, hoped his brother had made it safely home to the Diamond Buckle Saloon. There would be no finding out for a while, since the roads would be impassable.

He thought about Juliana, and how pleased she'd been when he'd shown her the bathtub. His mother had insisted on installing the thing, saying she was tired of heating water on the stove and bathing in the kitchen, ever fearful that some man would wander in and catch her in "the altogether."

At the time, he'd thought it was plain foolish, a waste of good money, but then Beth—destined to die in just a few short months—had pointed out that she'd had a bathtub of her very own back in Boston, and she missed it.

Lincoln had ridden to town the same day and placed an order at Willand's Mercantile. Weeks later, when the modern marvel arrived by train, shipped all the way from Denver in a crate big enough to house a grand piano, half the town had come out to the ranch to see it unloaded and set up in the smallest bedroom.

Husbands pulled Lincoln aside to complain; they were being hectored, they said. Now the wife wanted one of those infernal contraptions all her own.

He'd sympathized, and proffered that a bathtub with a boiler was a small price to pay for a peaceful household. Hell, it was worth the look of delighted disbelief he'd seen on Juliana's face when she saw it.

Guilt struck him again like the punch of a fist as he entered the barn, lit a lantern to see by so the work would go more quickly. He'd bought that bathtub for *Beth,* not Juliana.

The cow began to snuffle and snort, wanting to be milked.

Lincoln soothed her with a scratch between the ears and gave her hay instead. Once he'd fed all the horses and Wes's mule, he undertook the arduous task of hauling water from the well to fill the troughs.

By the time he'd finished that, milked and started back toward the house, bucket in hand, it was snowing again.

For a moment, Lincoln felt weary to the core of his spirit. Ranching was always hard work, always a risk, but in weather like this, with cattle on the range, it could be downright brutal.

Finding Juliana in the kitchen, and the coffee brewed, he felt better.

Tom was nowhere around, though, and that was unusual enough to worry Lincoln. He was about to ask if Juliana had seen him when Tom came out of his room just off the kitchen, tucking his flour-sack shirt into his pants.

"Too much reading," he said. "That Oliver feller has me worried."

Lincoln chuckled, poured himself some coffee. "What's for breakfast?" he asked. "Gruel?"

Tom looked puzzled, but Juliana smiled. "How about oatmeal?" she suggested brightly.

"No gruel?" Lincoln teased.

She laughed. "You haven't tasted my oatmeal."

The gruel, he soon discovered, would have been an improvement.

Joseph, turning up rumpled at the table, made a face when he saw it. "Is there any of that bear hash left?" he asked, his tone plaintive.

Only Tom accepted a second bowl of oatmeal.

When the three men left the house, they met Ben Gainer in the yard, and he looked worried. His freckles stood out against his pale face and his brownish-red hair stuck out in spikes under his hat. "Rose-of-Sharon is feelin' poorly this morning," he said.

"You'd better stay with her, then," Tom said quietly.

"I told her she ought to let you come and see if the baby's on its way, but she said—" Ben fell silent, blushed miserably. Turned his eyes to the snowy terrain and looked even grimmer than before.

All of them knew what Rose-of-Sharon Gainer had said. She didn't want an Indian tending her, no matter how "poorly" she might feel.

"It's all right, Ben," Tom told the boy. "Things get bad, you send Joseph out to the range to fetch me."

Glumly, stamping his feet to get the circulation going, Ben nodded, his breath making puffs of steam in the air, like their own. "With all this snow, I don't see how I could get to town to bring back the doctor."

Joseph had turned to Tom. "Don't I get to go with you? Out to the range?"

"Mike can do that. You'll stay here and help Art load the sled with hay."

There was a protest brewing in the boy's face, but it soon dissolved. He sighed and went on toward the barn.

They hauled the first load of hay out to the range half an hour later, and found the cattle in clusters, instinctively sharing their warmth and blocking the wind as best they could. The air they exhaled rose over them like smoke from a chimney.

The creek was slushy, but it flowed.

They went back to the barn for another load of feed, and then another. Tom scanned the surrounding plain for wolf or coyote tracks, and found none.

They headed back and met a panicked Joseph, all but stuck in snow reaching to his midthighs and waving both arms.

Lincoln, driving the team while Tom rode behind him on the sled, felt a sinking sensation in the pit of his stomach.

The boy shouted something, but Lincoln couldn't

make out the words. It didn't matter. Something was wrong, that was all he needed to know.

He drove the draft horses harder, and Tom scrambled off the sled and crow-hopped his way through the snow toward the boy.

Chapter Five

Lincoln heard the screams as he left the horses with Joseph to be unhitched, led to their stalls, rubbed down and fed. He followed Tom toward the cabin out by the bunkhouse, moving as fast as he could.

Glancing once toward the main house, he saw Gracie and Theresa standing at the window, both their faces pale with worry.

The cabin was only about eight by eight feet, so it was impossible to overlook the straining form in the center of the bed. Juliana was seated nearby, holding Rose-of-

Sharon Gainer's hand and speaking softly, and the sight of her calmed Lincoln a little.

Nothing was going to calm Ben, though.

He paced at the foot of the bed, frenzied, shoving both hands through his hair every few steps. He looked like a wild man, some hermit from the high timber, baffled by his new surroundings.

"You go on over to the big house," Tom told the young husband firmly. "You'll be of no help to us here."

Ben set his jaw, glanced at his weeping, sweating wife, and looked as though he might throw a punch. Finally, though, he bent over Rose-of-Sharon, kissed her forehead and did as he'd been told, putting on his coat, passing Lincoln without a word or a look and closing the cabin door smartly behind him.

Lincoln, unsure of whether to stay or follow right on Ben's heels, stood just inside the door, turning his gaze to the pitiful little Christmas tree with its strands of colored yarn and awkwardly cut paper ornaments. Two packages, wrapped in brown paper and tied with coarse twine, lay bravely beneath it.

"Breathe very slowly, Rose-of-Sharon," he heard Juliana say, her voice soft and even, but underlaid with a tone of worry.

Lincoln slowed his own breathing, since the idea seemed like a good one.

"You'll be all right," Tom told the girl.

Rose-of-Sharon, a pretty thing with glossy brown hair, was well beyond fussing over letting an Indian attend her. "Is—is the doctor coming?" she asked, between long, low moans and ragged breaths it hurt to hear.

Lincoln thought of the snow, so deep now that the draft horses had had all they could do to get through it, plodding to and fro as they hauled hay to the cattle.

"Yes," Tom lied, rolling up his sleeves and inclining his head slightly in Juliana's direction. "He's on his way for sure."

An unspoken signal must have gone from Tom to Juliana. She nodded and raised the bedclothes.

The sheets and Rose-of-Sharon's nightgown were crimson.

Lincoln turned his back, busied himself building up the fire in the little stove that served for both cooking and heating the cabin. Because the chinking between the logs of the structure was good and the ceiling was low, the room would stay warm.

Rose-of-Sharon shrieked, and the sound scraped down

Lincoln's insides like a claw. For a few moments, it was Beth lying in that bed, not Ben Gainer's child-bride.

He wondered again if he ought to leave, get out from underfoot the way Ben had, but something held him there. He'd go if Tom told him to; otherwise, he'd remain. Do what he could, which was probably precious little.

"Put some water on to heat," Tom said from the fraught void behind Lincoln. "Then go to the house for my medicine bag."

Lincoln nodded—no words would come out—found a kettle, went outside to pack it full of snow, since the water bucket was empty, and set it on the stove. He carried the bucket to the well next, worked to fill it, carried it back inside. Next, he made his way to the house, frustrated by the slow going, found all the kids and Ben gathered at the kitchen table, staring down at their hands.

For some reason, the sight left him stricken, unable to move for a few moments. When he managed to break the spell, he headed for Tom's room, really more of a lean-to, and grabbed the familiar buckskin pouch from its place under the narrow bed. Joseph's pallet, fashioned of folded quilts and blankets, lay crumpled against the inside wall.

Leaving the room, he nearly collided with Ben.

"Rose-of-Sharon?" Ben asked, his voice hoarse, his eyes hollow with quiet frenzy.

"Too soon to know," Lincoln said, and sidestepped past him.

"I'm going for the doctor," Ben said, following him to the back door.

Lincoln turned. "No," he said. "You'd never make it that far, and even if you did, old Doc Chaney wouldn't budge in this weather."

"My wife could die!"

Lincoln looked past him, his gaze connecting with Gracie's. She was white with terror, no doubt remembering Beth's passing, and he longed to go to her, assure her everything would be all right.

The problem was, it might not.

Lincoln laid a hand on Ben's shoulder. "Yes," he said gravely, because nothing but the stark truth would have done. "She could die. But there's no point in your freezing to death somewhere between here and Stillwater Springs, whether she does or not. Besides, if Rose-of-Sharon and the baby survive this, they'll need you."

Ben considered that, swallowed hard and gave a grudging nod.

Lincoln turned and bolted out the door, wading hard for the cabin, the long strap of Tom's medicine pouch pressing heavy into his shoulder.

JULIANA HAD NEVER, in the whole of her life, been so frightened. At the same time, she was oddly calm, as though another self had risen within her, pushed the schoolmarm aside and taken over.

The scene was nightmarish, with all that blood, and poor Rose-of-Sharon shrieking as though she were being torn apart from the inside.

When Lincoln returned with the bag Tom had sent him for, Tom took the bag, plundered it, solemn-faced, then brought out a smaller pouch with strange markings burned into it. His own hands covered in blood, he extended the pouch to Juliana and instructed her to put a pinch of the seeds under Rose-of-Sharon's tongue.

Trembling, she obeyed.

"Don't swallow," Tom told the girl. "It'll ease the pain some, in a few minutes, and then we'll see about getting that baby born."

"Am I going to die?" Rose-of-Sharon pleaded, her eyes ricocheting between Juliana and Tom. She looked so small and so young—no more than fifteen or thereabouts. It was only too common for girls of her station to marry at an early age. "Is my baby going to die?"

Tom spoke in the Indian way, some of his syllables flat. "No," he said, with such certainty that Juliana glanced up at him. She saw the determination in his face, at once placid and stalwart. "But this could take a while. You'll have to be as brave as you can."

Rose-of-Sharon bit down hard on her lower lip, nodded, her skin glistening with perspiration, her eyes catching Juliana's, begging. *Hold on tight,* they seemed to say. *Don't let me go.*

"I'm here," Juliana said, in the same tone she'd used when one of the children was sick or frightened in the night. She squeezed Rose-of-Sharon's small hand. "I'm right here, Rose-of-Sharon, and I'm not going anywhere."

The words, spoken so quietly, were at complete odds with her every instinct. Given her druthers, Juliana would have jumped up and run out into the snow, turning in blind, frantic circles, gasping at air and screaming until her throat was raw.

What was calming her?

Surely, it was necessity, at least in part. Tom's quiet confidence helped, too. In the main, though, it was knowing Lincoln was there, feeling his presence through the skin of her back, as surely as she felt the heat from the stove.

He seemed as strong and immovable as any of the mountains rising skyward in the distance.

Tom asked for a basin, once the water had been heated, and instructed Lincoln to prepare more. Juliana bathed Rose-of-Sharon, helped her into her spare nightgown, while Tom removed the soiled sheets, replacing them with a blanket.

And Rose-of-Sharon's travails continued.

Between keening screeches of pain, her body straining mightily, she rested, eyes closed, pale lips moving constantly in wordless prayer or protest.

The light shifted, dimmed, became shadow-laced.

Lincoln lit lanterns. Left the cabin again to make sure the children were all right and the barn chores got done.

Juliana, as preoccupied with tending to Rose-of-Sharon as she was, barely breathed until he came back.

It was well into the night when the crisis finally

came; too exhausted to scream, Rose-of-Sharon convulsed instead, her eyes rolling back into her head, her back curved high off the mattress in an impossible arch.

The baby slipped from her then, a tiny, bluish creature, soundless and still.

Tom caught the little form in his cupped hands.

Was the child dead? Juliana waited to know, felt Lincoln waiting, too.

And then Tom smiled, grabbed up one of the discarded blankets and wrapped the baby in a clean corner of the cloth. "Welcome, little man," he said. "Welcome."

The infant boy squalled, such a small sound. So full of life and power.

Tears slipped down Juliana's cheeks.

Rose-of-Sharon, spent as she was, seemed lit from within, like a Madonna. She reached out for the baby, and Tom laid him gently in her arms.

"Get Ben," Rose-of-Sharon murmured. "Please get my Ben."

Juliana heard the door open as Lincoln rushed to do the girl's bidding, felt a rush of cold air, and shielded mother and child from the draft as best she could. Only minutes later, Lincoln returned with the new father.

Ben approached the bed slowly, a man enthralled, hardly daring to believe his own eyes.

"Come see," Rose-of-Sharon said, the last shreds of her strength going into her wobbly smile. "Come and see your son, Ben Gainer."

The room seemed to tilt all of the sudden, and the world went dark. Juliana was barely aware of being lifted out of her chair next to the bed, bundled tightly into her cloak, lifted into strong arms.

Lincoln's arms.

She felt his coat enfold her, too, the way it had in the wagon, on the way out from town. "I've got to stay," she managed to say, blinking against the blinding fatigue that had risen up around her between one moment and the next. "They'll need—"

"Hush," Lincoln said.

Even in the bitter cold, she felt only the warmth of him as he carried her through the snow and into the main house. A single lantern burned in the middle of the kitchen table, but the room was empty. What time was it?

"The children…?"

"Theresa put them to bed hours ago," Lincoln said, making no move to set her on her feet. Instead, he took her through the house, along the corridor, into a room several doors down from hers.

He laid her on the bed, covered her quickly with a quilt, tucked it in tightly around her.

The fatigue reached deep into her mind, into her very marrow. She tried to get a handhold on consciousness, but the strange darkness kept swallowing her down again.

She was aware of Lincoln moving about, now removing her shoes, now opening a bureau drawer.

"Lincoln?" she asked, scrambling back up the monster's throat only to be swallowed once more.

She knew when he left the room, knew when he came back, after what seemed like a long time, but could not have said which of her senses had alerted her to the leaving and the returning. She could not seem to fix on anything; she wasn't asleep, and yet she wasn't fully awake, either.

Lincoln was lifting her again, carrying her again, still cocooned in the quilt. When had she last felt so safe, so cared-for? Surely not since early childhood, when she'd had two loving parents and a brother.

"Where…?"

"Shh," he said.

The sound of running water and the misty caress of steam roused her a little. Lincoln stood her on her feet, supporting her with one arm, peeling away her clothes with the other hand.

He was *undressing* her.

But suddenly it seemed the most normal thing in the world for him to be doing. There was no fear in her, no resistance.

He helped her into the bathtub, and the warmth of the water, the soothing, blessed heat, encompassed her. Of course, she thought, drifting. She'd been soaked in poor Rose-of-Sharon's blood.

Her dress had surely been ruined, and she could not spare it.

Helpless tears welled in her eyes.

"My dress," she lamented in a despairing whisper. In that moment, she was grieving over so much more than the best of her three calico gowns. Her mother, her father. Grandmama and Clay. She had lost them all, and she could bear no more of such losing.

"There are other dresses," Lincoln told her, lifting her again, drying off her bare skin with soft swipes of a rough towel, pulling a nightgown on over her head. It felt soft and worn, and the scent—rosewater and talcum powder—was not her own.

Supporting her with one arm around her waist—*why* was she so weak?—he guided her out into the corridor again. Past the door to the room she'd been sharing with Billy-Moses and Daisy.

"The children," she protested.

"Theresa's with them," he told her.

He took her back to his room—a slight, wicked thrill flickered through her at the realization—and put her into his bed.

She began to weep, with weariness and with relief, because, out in the little cabin, sorrow had drawn so near and then passed on. For now.

Lincoln sat down on the edge of the mattress. Kicked off his boots. In the next moment, he was under the covers with her, fully clothed, holding her close. Just then, Juliana knew only two things: she'd be ruined for sure, and she'd die if he let her go.

He did not let her go—several times during the night, she awakened, gradually growing more coherent, and felt his arms around her, felt his chest warm beneath her cheek.

When she opened her eyes the next time, all weariness gone, she found herself looking straight into Lincoln's face. By the thinning darkness, she knew dawn would be breaking soon.

"Since we just spent the night in the same bed," Lincoln said reasonably, as though they'd been discussing the subject for hours and now he was putting his foot down, "I think we'd better get married."

Juliana stared at him, her eyes widening until they hurt. "Married?"

He merely smiled.

She swallowed. "But—surely—"

The door creaked open. "Papa?" Gracie's voice chimed. "Theresa can't find Miss Mitchell and—"

Juliana wanted to pull the covers up over her head, hide, but it was too late. Gracie, fleet as a fairy, was beside the bed now.

"Oh," she said, in a tone of merry innocence, "*there* you are!"

"Gracie—" Lincoln began.

But she cut him off by shouting, "Theresa! I found Miss Mitchell! She's right here in Papa's bed!"

Juliana groaned.

Lincoln laughed. "Miss Mitchell has something to tell you, Gracie," he said.

"What?" Gracie asked curiously.

Juliana drew a very deep breath, let it out slowly. "Your father and I are getting married," she said.

"I'm going to have a mama?" Gracie enthused. "That's even better than a *dictionary!*"

"You go on back to bed now," Lincoln told his daughter.

She obeyed with surprising alacrity, fairly dancing through the shadows toward the door.

"That," Juliana told Lincoln, in a righteous whisper, "was a *very* underhanded thing to do."

He sat up, clothes rumpled, swung his legs over the side of the bed, then leaned to pull his boots back on. He was humming under his breath, a sound like muted laughter, or creek water burbling along under a spring sky.

"Soon as the snow melts off a little," he said, as though she hadn't spoken at all, "I'll send for somebody to marry us. Probably be the justice of the peace, since the circuit preacher only comes through when the spirit moves him."

She could have protested, but for some reason, she didn't.

Lincoln added wood to the hearth fire and got it crackling again. "You might as well go back to sleep," he said. "Rest up a little."

Juliana lay there, the covers pulled up to her chin, and reviewed what had just happened. She'd accepted a proposal of marriage—of sorts. It was as unlike what she'd imagined, both as a girl and as a grown woman, as it could possibly have been.

It was all wrong.

It was wildly *un*romantic.

Why, then, did she feel this peculiar, taut-string excitement, this desire to sing?

Sleeping proved impossible. The children were up; she could hear their voices and footsteps. Besides, she was rested.

She must get dressed, do something with her hair, put on her cloak and go out to the cabin to look in on Rose-of-Sharon and the baby. Suppose the fire had gone out and they took a chill?

Rising, she realized that yesterday's calico, no doubt beyond salvaging anyhow, had disappeared. A pretty blue woolen frock with black piping lay across the foot of the bed—Lincoln's doing, she reflected with a blush. A garment his wife must have owned, since it did not look matronly enough to belong to his mother, as the oversize nightgown probably did.

For a moment, she considered her remaining dresses, both frayed at the seams and oft-mended, both worn threadbare. Both inadequate for winter weather.

She put on the lovely blue woolen, buttoned it up the front. Except at the bosom, where it was a little too tight, it fit remarkably well.

The children, she soon discovered, had assembled in the kitchen. Seated around the table, they all stared at her as though she'd grown horns during the night. Lincoln was making breakfast—eggs and hotcakes—and Tom was just stepping through the back door, stomping snow off his boots.

Juliana forgot her embarrassment. "Rose-of-Sharon?" she asked, her breath catching. "How is she? How is the baby?"

Tom's smile flashed, bright as sunshine on snow. "She's just fine, and so is the little man," he said. "I don't reckon she'd mind some female company, though."

Juliana nodded, looking back at the children. "No lessons today," she said. With the exception of Gracie, they looked delighted. "And I expect you all to behave yourselves."

They all nodded solemnly, from Joseph right on down to Billy-Moses and Daisy. Their eyes were huge, though whether that was due to the blue dress or the fact that she'd spent the night in Lincoln Creed's bedroom and everyone in the household seemed to know it, she could not begin to say.

She looked about for her cloak, realized that it had probably been hopelessly stained, like her dress.

"Take my coat," Lincoln said.

Juliana hesitated, then lifted the long and surprisingly heavy black coat from its peg and put it on, nearly enveloped by it. With one hand, she held up the hem, so she wouldn't trip or drag the cloth on the ground.

She stepped outside into the first timorous light of day, and immediately noticed that the eaves were dripping. The snow was slushy beneath her feet.

Would Lincoln ride to town and fetch back the justice of the peace, now that the weather was changing? A quivery, delicious dread overtook her as she hurried toward the Gainers' cabin. Light glowed in the single window, and smoke curled from the stovepipe chimney.

She *could* refuse to marry Lincoln, of course—even though she'd slept in his room, in his *bed,* nothing untoward had taken place. Why, he hadn't even kissed her.

She blushed furiously and walked faster, remembering the bath, trying to outdistance the recollection. He'd undressed her, seen her naked flesh, *washed* her. At the time, she had been too dazed by exhaustion and the delivery of Rose-of-Sharon's baby to protest. The experience hadn't seemed—well—*real.*

Now, however, she felt the slickness of the soap, the heat of the water, the tender touch of Lincoln's hand, just as if it were all happening right then. She quickened her steps again, but the sensations kept up with her.

It was a relief when Ben Gainer opened the cabin door to greet her, smiling from ear to ear.

"Rose-of-Sharon's been asking for you," he said.

Juliana hurried inside so the door could be closed against the soggy chill of the morning. A fire crackled in the stove, and the cabin was cozy, scented with fresh coffee and just-baked biscuits. Even the pitiful little Christmas tree had taken on a certain scruffy splendor. Rose-of-Sharon sat up in bed, pillows plumped behind her back, nursing her baby behind a draped blanket.

The girl's face shone with a light all her own, and Juliana felt a swift pang of pure envy.

Ben took Lincoln's coat from Juliana's shoulders and told her to help herself to coffee and biscuits, explaining that Tom had done the baking.

"I'll be back as soon as we've fed those cattle," he added, putting on his own coat and hat and leaving the cabin.

Ravenous, Juliana poured coffee into a mug, took a steaming biscuit from the covered pan on top of the stove. She sat beside the bed, in last night's chair, while she ate.

When she'd finished nursing the baby, Rose-of-Sharon righted her nightgown and lowered the quilt to show Juliana her son. He was wrapped in a pretty crocheted blanket.

He seemed impossibly small, frighteningly delicate. His skin was very nearly translucent.

"Do you want to hold him?" Rose-of-Sharon asked when Juliana had finished the biscuit and brushed fallen crumbs from the skirt of the blue dress.

The only thing greater than Juliana's trepidation was her desire to take that baby into her arms. Carefully, she did so, her heart beating a little faster.

"My mama sent that blanket," Rose-of-Sharon said.

"All the way from Cheyenne. Ben says he'll take me and the baby home to Wyoming for a visit come spring so we can show him off to the family."

The baby gave an infinitesimal hiccup. He weighed no more than a feather. "Have you given him a name?"

Rose-of-Sharon smiled. "I wanted to call him Benjamin, for his daddy, but Ben'll have none of it. Never liked the name much. So we picked one out of the Good Book—Joshua."

"Joshua," Juliana repeated softly. She pictured the walls of Jericho tumbling down. "That's a fine, strong name."

"Joshua Thomas Gainer," Rose-of-Sharon said.

Juliana looked up.

"Yes," Rose-of-Sharon told her. "For Tom Dancingstar. Did Ben tell you I didn't want him looking after me, because it ain't proper for an Indian to tend a white woman?"

Juliana didn't speak. She did shake her head, though. Ben hadn't told her, and she was glad.

"If Joshua had been a girl," Rose-of-Sharon went on, more softly now, holding out her arms for the baby again, "I'd have chosen your name." She wrinkled her brow curiously, and Juliana, surrendering Joshua with some reluctance, thought of Angelique, wondered if she and Blue Johnston had gotten married. "What *is* your name, anyhow?"

She laughed. "Juliana."

"That's right pretty."

"Thank you. So is Rose-of-Sharon."

Rose-of-Sharon blushed a little. "I'm obliged to you," she said. "The hardest thing about having a baby was being so far from Mama—or at least that's what I thought until it started hurting."

Juliana smiled, tucked the blankets in more snugly around both Rose-of-Sharon and the baby. "You'll forget the pain with time," she said.

"I ain't yet," Rose-of-Sharon said devoutly, and with a little shudder for emphasis. She yawned, and her eyelids drooped a little. "I'm plum worn down to a nubbin," she added.

"Get some rest," Juliana urged gently.

"What if I roll over on Joshua while I'm sleeping?" Rose-of-Sharon fretted. "He's such a little thing."

"I'll make sure you don't," Juliana promised. There was no cradle, but she spotted a small chest of drawers in a corner of the cabin. Removing one drawer, she lined it with a folded quilt, set it next to the bed where Rose-of-Sharon could see and reach, and carefully placed the baby inside.

With no more quilts or blankets on hand, Juliana used several of Ben's heavy flannel shirts to cover little Joshua.

Satisfied that her baby was safe, Rose-of-Sharon slept.

Juliana sat quietly through the morning, her mood introspective.

At half past one that afternoon, the men returned, chilled and red-faced from the brisk wind, and Ben took over the care of his wife and son.

Juliana wore Lincoln's coat, and as they stood in front of the cabin door, he carefully did up the buttons, his gloved hands, smelling of hay, lingering on the collar, close against her face.

"Tom will ride to town and ask after the justice of the peace," he said, "if you're agreeable to that."

Juliana gazed up at him. She had not had time to fall in love with this man—he certainly hadn't swept her off her feet, not in the romantic sense, anyway—but she respected him. She *liked* him.

Was that enough?

It seemed that someone else spoke up in her place. "I'm agreeable," she said.

His smile was so sudden, so dazzling, that it nearly knocked her back on her heels. "Good," he said huskily. "That's good."

A cloud crossed an inner sun. "This—this dress—"

"Beth's mother sent crates full of them, every so often," he told her, his eyes gentle, perceptive. "She never got around to wearing it."

Juliana absorbed that, nodded.

Lincoln took her hand. "Let's get that Christmas tree set up," he said with a laugh, "before Gracie pesters me into an early grave."

Minutes later, while Juliana and the children took boxes of delicate ornaments from the shelves of a small storage room off the parlor, Lincoln went to the woodshed to get the tree, Joseph right on his heels.

It was so big that it took both of them to wrestle it through the front door, its branches exuding the piney scent Juliana had always associated with Christmas.

Billy-Moses and Daisy stared at the tree in wonder, huddled so close together that their shoulders touched, and holding hands. Juliana remembered Mr. Philbert, and knew in a flash of certainty that he would come for them one day soon.

Tears filled her eyes.

She would be Mrs. Lincoln Creed by then, most likely, and with a husband to take her part, it wasn't likely she'd be arrested. Still, when Mr. Philbert took Daisy and Billy-Moses away, it would be as if he'd torn out her heart and dragged it, bruised and bouncing, down the road behind his departing buggy.

"Juliana?"

She looked up, surprised to see Lincoln standing directly in front of her.

He cupped her elbows in the palms of his hands, kissed her forehead. "Let them have Christmas," he said.

Either he was extremely perceptive, or he'd seen the worry in her face.

She nodded. Dashed at her eyes with the back of one hand.

It took all afternoon to festoon that Christmas tree, and what a magnificent sight it was, bedecked in ribbon garlands, delicate blown-glass ornaments of all shapes and colors, draped with shimmering strands of tinsel. Even Juliana, who had grown up in a Denver mansion with an even grander tree erected in her grandmother's library every December, was awestruck.

Tom appeared at dusk, while Lincoln was doing the chores in the barn. He carried a large white package under one arm.

Juliana, peeling potatoes and trying to think what else to prepare for supper, couldn't help looking past him to see if he'd brought the justice of the peace along.

She was both relieved and disappointed to see that he was alone.

He smiled, as though he'd read her thoughts again, and set the parcel on the counter. "Chickens," he said. "All cut up and ready to fry."

Mildly embarrassed, Juliana reported that she'd looked in on Rose-of-Sharon and little Joshua earlier, and they were doing well.

Moving to the sink to wash his hands, Tom nodded. Although, since his back was turned to her, and Juliana couldn't be sure, she thought he was smiling to himself.

He brought lard and a big skillet from the pantry, set the pan to warming on the stove, then rolled the chicken parts in a bowl of flour. They worked in companionable silence, Juliana finishing up the potatoes and putting them on to boil.

The savory sizzle of frying chicken soon brought the children in from the front room, where they'd been admiring the Christmas tree.

"We'll need an extra place set at the table," Tom commented mildly, after Theresa had counted out plates and silverware for everyone. His dark eyes twinkled as Juliana turned to him. "For the circuit preacher. He's out in the barn with Lincoln."

Juliana nearly gasped aloud, and before she could think of a response, the back door opened and Lincoln came in, closely followed by a very large white-haired man in austere black clothes and a clerical collar.

The circuit preacher's eyes were a pale, merry blue, in startling contrast to his sober garments, and before Lincoln could make an introduction, he lumbered over to Juliana like a great, good-natured bear, one hand stuck out in greeting.

"This must be the bride!" he boomed.

Juliana's face flamed. She fidgeted, unable to meet Lincoln's gaze, and shook the reverend's hand.

Gracie piped up. "This morning when I went into Papa's room—"

Theresa put one palm over the child's mouth just in time.

The reverend turned to look at Tom, drawing in an appreciative breath. "Is that fried chicken I smell?"

Tom laughed, nodded.

"And me just in time for supper!" the reverend roared.

Just then, Daisy crept up beside the big man and tugged at the sleeve of his coat. "Are you Saint Nicholas?" she asked, almost breathless with her own daring.

The reverend bellowed out a great guffaw at that. Daisy started, but didn't retreat.

"Why, bless your heart, child," the preacher thundered, "nobody's ever mistaken this ole Bible-pounder for a saint!"

"That's Reverend Dettly, silly goose," Gracie informed Daisy solicitously. "Saint Nicholas always wears red."

"You'll spend the night, won't you, Reverend?" Lincoln asked, taking the preacher's coat. "It's dark out there, and mighty cold, even with the thaw."

"I reckon I'll burrow into a hay pile out in your barn, all right," Reverend Dettly said. "A belly full of ole Tom's chicken ought to keep me plenty warm."

"Surely we can offer you a bed," Juliana said shyly.

Reverend Dettly smiled down at her. "I won't be putting anybody out of their beds," he said. "If a stable was good enough for our Lord, it's sure as all get-out good enough for me."

Chapter Six

Tom took plates out to the cabin for Ben and Rose-of-Sharon as soon as supper was ready. When he returned, everyone was already seated around the table, Reverend Dettly waiting patiently to offer up the blessing.

Juliana sat at Lincoln's right side, stomach jittering with fearful anticipation and hunger. Soon, she would be his *wife*. Mrs. Lincoln Creed. Would he expect her to share his bed that night, or would he give her time to get used to being married?

Did she *want* time to get used to it?

The reverend cleared his throat once Tom had joined them, held out his great pawlike hands and closed his eyes to deliver the longest and most exuberant blessing Juliana had ever heard. Behind closed eyelids, her head dutifully bowed, she imagined the gravy congealing, the mountainous piles of fried chicken going cold, and still the preacher went on, thanking God for everything he could think of, from seeds germinating in the earth under their blanket of snow, to the cattle on a thousand hills. When someone's stomach rumbled loudly and at length, Dettly laughed and shouted a joyful "Amen!"

"Thank God," Lincoln agreed.

Juliana elbowed him.

During that meal, it seemed there were two Julianas—one seated next to Lincoln at the table, laughing and talking and enjoying the savory food, and one standing back a ways at the edge of the lantern light, wringing her hands and fretting.

"So," the reverend said, turning to Juliana when he'd eaten his third and apparently final helping of everything, "I'm told there's to be a wedding. I've known Lincoln here since he couldn't see over the top of a water trough, but I don't believe I've ever made the bride's acquaintance."

Juliana felt her cheeks warm, and it took some doing to meet that direct blue gaze, kindly but penetrating, too, head-on. She told him her name, though Tom had probably done that long since, and that she'd been the teacher at the Indian School until it closed down.

"You look good and sturdy," the preacher observed, as though she were a calf he might buy at a stock sale.

Juliana wasn't offended, but she *was* amused. "I have good teeth, too," she said with a twinkle.

Reverend Dettly laughed, but his eyes took on an expression of solemnity as he continued to regard her. "You're amenable to this, Miss Mitchell? Getting married is a serious thing, with eternal consequences. Mustn't be too hasty about it."

Was having no other viable choice the same as being amenable? Juliana didn't know. Her heart seemed to be getting bigger and bigger, sure to burst at any time, and it all but cut off the breath she needed to answer.

"I'm willing to marry Mr. Creed," she said. Even if she didn't get arrested, Mr. Philbert would probably see that she never taught in any school again. If she went home to Denver, it would be on Clay's terms, and she would essentially be a prisoner. She imagined herself growing more and more eccentric as the years passed, until she finally ended up wild-eyed and confined to the attic.

The thought made her shudder.

The children were unusually quiet. Juliana couldn't hear the big wall clock ticking, though she knew it was because she'd climbed up onto a stool and wound it herself earlier with a brass key.

"Very well," the reverend said, evidently satisfied, "let's get on with it, then." In remote areas like Stillwater Springs, Montana, where loneliness and hard work were the order of the day, he probably performed the marriage ceremony for all sorts of unromantic reasons.

Juliana cast a look up and down the table. "As soon as we've washed the dishes—"

"Hang the dishes," Lincoln said, taking her by the hand and pulling her to her feet. "Let's get this thing *done.*" With that, he all but dragged her into the front room, the children and Tom following single file like goslings, Reverend Dettly bringing up the rear.

Lincoln stood with his back to the Christmas tree, Juliana at his side. Suddenly, it seemed to her that the whole scene was taking place under water, or inside one of those pretty crystal globes that produced snow flurries when they were shaken. Dettly pulled a small, oft-used prayer book from the pocket of his suit coat, cleared his throat ponderously.

Tom and Joseph were appointed as witnesses; Gracie insisted on being one, too.

The ceremony was amazingly brief; Juliana heard it all through a dull pounding in her ears, responded whenever Lincoln squeezed her hand. The reverend had to repeat himself a lot.

There were no rings and no flowers.

The dress Juliana wore belonged to someone else, and was too tight in the bodice.

For all that, she felt cautiously hopeful, if dazed, and perhaps even happy.

Reverend Dettly pronounced them man and wife, and that, Juliana thought, was that. Until Lincoln turned her to face him, cupped his hands on either side of her face and kissed her so soundly that she had to grasp at his shirt to keep herself from floating away.

When that kiss was over, Juliana stared up into her husband's face, confounded by all he'd made her feel. Fiery sparks leaped within her, and there was this odd sense of *expansion,* embarrassingly physical but going well beyond that into realms of mind and spirit she had never previously comprehended, let alone explored.

The earth shifted beneath her feet, heaven trembled above her.

She was different.

Everything was different.

Lincoln frowned slightly, looking puzzled and a little concerned. "Are you all right?" he asked.

She nodded. Shook her head. Sagged a little, as though she might swoon—she who had *never* swooned until last night, after helping with a difficult birth—causing Lincoln to slip an arm around her.

"Juliana?"

"I'm—we're—married," she said stupidly.

Lincoln's concern softened into a smile. "Yes," he said.

Gracie tugged at the skirt of Juliana's dress. "May I call you Mama now, please?" she asked.

Juliana's heart turned over; she glanced at Lincoln, but saw no urging, one way or the other, in his face. They were strangers to each other, she and Lincoln, and the decision to marry had been made out of expediency on Lincoln's part and desperation on her own. Suppose, in a month or a year, they found they could not tolerate each other? Gracie, thinking of Juliana as a mother, would be crushed.

Looking down into those hopeful eyes, though, Juliana knew she couldn't refuse. "Yes, darling," she said softly. "If you want to call me Mama, you may. But you had another mother—wasn't she 'Mama'?"

"Does a person only get one mama?" Gracie asked, looking worried.

Juliana was at a complete loss. She and Gracie both turned to Lincoln for an answer. He looked flummoxed.

Gracie took charge. "My first mama died," she said. "I loved her—she was pretty and she smelled nice—but she's gone. I won't see her again until I get to heaven, and that might be a long, long time from now. So I need another mama to get me through till then."

Juliana's eyes stung, but she smiled. She couldn't help it; Gracie had her thoroughly bewitched. "All right, then," she said, praying she would never have to let this trusting child down. "It's a bargain. I'll be the best mama I can."

Gracie wasn't finished. Placing her hands on her hips, she said, "Theresa told me that she and Joseph are going home to North Dakota as soon as they can raise the train fare. Couldn't Billy-Moses and Daisy stay here with us and be Creeds, too?"

Juliana closed her eyes.

"Go and help with the washing up," Lincoln told his daughter mildly.

"But you didn't *answer* me, Papa."

"Go."

She left, the reverend in tow, and Juliana and Lincoln were alone, as a married couple, for the first time. The tree sparkled behind Lincoln; a strand of tinsel caught in his hair. Without thinking, Juliana reached up to remove that thin silvery strip, draped it on the closest branch. Her touch was tender.

She'd done a fairly good job of setting aside her fears for the youngest of her charges, but now Gracie's question echoed in her heart like the peal of distant church bells. *Couldn't Billy-Moses and Daisy stay here with us and be Creeds, too?*

"What happens now?" she asked, unable to hold the words back any longer.

Lincoln put his arms around her waist loosely and drew her closer. Ducked his head to kiss the tip of her nose. "Now," he said throatily, "we take things slowly. I want you in my bed, Juliana Creed, I won't deny it. But I won't ask you for anything you're not ready to give—you have my word on that."

Juliana Creed. That was who she was now. It seemed remarkable, as though she'd lived all her life as one person and then suddenly turned into another. As she looked up at Lincoln, she wondered if what she felt—the crazy tangle of longing and sweet sorrow and myriad other things too new to be named—might be love.

Surely that was impossible. She had only known Lincoln for a few days—how could she have learned to love him in such a short period of time?

"I'm—I'm not sure when I'll be ready, Lincoln," she confessed. "I've never— I mean, John and I didn't—wouldn't have—"

He ran a hand lightly down the length of her braid, gave it a gentle tug. "We'll take our time, Juliana," he reiterated. A sparkle lit his brown eyes. "Not too *much* time, mind you."

A lovely shiver went through her, but then she remembered tales she'd heard other women relate, concerning intimate things that happened between a man and a woman, and frowned.

"What?" Lincoln asked. How he favored that one-word question. He was not one for long speeches, that was for sure.

Juliana flushed with tender misery. "Will it hurt?"

Gently, he ran the backs of his fingers along her cheek. "Maybe a little, the first time or two. But I'll be careful, Juliana. That's a promise."

She believed him. She might not know Lincoln Creed very well, but there *were* things she was sure of where he was concerned. Many men would have packed Gracie off to live with relatives after her mother died—Juliana's own father, for instance—or shipped her away to some distant boarding school, but he'd kept her at home. He clearly loved his daughter, but she wasn't spoiled. He'd brought a strange woman and four Indian children into his home, just because they'd needed someplace to go. He'd stood by, ready to do whatever he could to help, while a young wife gave birth to her first child amid screams and blood, and every morning, without fail, no matter how bitterly cold the weather, he rose before dawn and made sure the range cattle didn't go hungry.

Rising on tiptoe, she kissed his cheek, felt the stubble of a beard against her lips. "I'd better put Daisy and Billy-

Moses to bed," she said. "Would you mind if I gave them a bath first?"

Lincoln smiled, touched her lower lip with the tip of one finger. "This is your house, too, Mrs. Creed. You don't have to ask permission to use the bathtub or anything else I own."

A niggle of worry snaked along the bottom of Juliana's stomach. "Speaking of Mrs. Creed," she said, after working up her courage, "what will your mother say when she finds out you've taken a wife?"

"I don't really care," Lincoln replied easily. "My guess is she'll be a little testy for a while, thinking I ought to have consulted her first, and then she'll get to know you better and come to like you. Anyhow, she won't be back from Phoenix for months—she hates the cold weather, and every year she threatens to stay there for good, since there's no 'culture' in Stillwater Springs, and she dreads being stuck out here on the ranch for weeks at a time. I think the only reason she comes back at all is because she's afraid Gracie will grow up to cuss, chew tobacco and wear pants if she's left with Tom and me for too long at a stretch."

Juliana smiled at the image of Gracie acting like a man.

One thing was for certain; Gracie Creed would never be ordinary. "*I* think you and Tom have done a fine job making a home for that little girl."

He grinned, gave her braid one more tug. "I'll go light a fire in the boiler and make sure there's water for a bath," he said. With that, he turned and walked away.

Juliana watched him until he'd vanished into the corridor on the other side of the front room, then took herself to the kitchen.

Tom and the reverend were doing up the dishes while Joseph read aloud from *Oliver Twist.* Theresa was wiping the table with a damp cloth while Gracie sat on the floor near the stove, entertaining Daisy and Billy-Moses with the alphabet blocks.

"That's your name," she said, lining up the blocks to spell *Daisy.*

Daisy stared at the letters in uncomprehending wonder. She was only three, after all. Gracie, with her bright hair and agile mind, must have seemed like a living oracle to her.

"Make *Bill,*" Billy-Moses urged.

"It's time for your bath," Juliana interceded.

Daisy, who loved baths, was on her feet in a moment. Billy-Moses's small face took on an obstinate expression.

"I don't *want* a bath," he said, folding his arms.

Reverend Dettly turned from the sink, his big hands dripping with suds, smiling. It struck Juliana that his life was probably a very solitary one when he wasn't preaching, but traveling from place to place and sleeping in people's barns. No doubt he enjoyed evenings like this one, being around children and eating a home-cooked meal.

"This is not a question of what you want, Billy-Moses," Juliana said firmly. "You *are* going to have a bath, and then you are going to bed. Period."

"Are you going to sleep in Papa's room again tonight?" Gracie asked innocently. This time, Theresa hadn't been close enough to cover her mouth.

Juliana's face flamed, and she couldn't have looked at Reverend Dettly to save her very life. "Yes," she said, because there was nothing else *to* say.

Lincoln had to pump and carry water to fill the boiler over the bathtub, and then it had to heat. When it was finally ready, Juliana bathed Daisy first with Theresa's help, put her to bed and went in search of Billy-Moses.

By that time, Reverend Dettly had retired to the barn,

and Tom and Joseph to their shared room off the kitchen. Only Lincoln was there, seated at the table, reading a newspaper.

"Have you seen…?" she began.

"He's hiding in the pantry behind the flour bin," Lincoln said, taking in his harried bride. The front of the marvelous blue dress was soaked from Daisy's happy splashing in the tub, and her hair was popping out of the braid like a frayed rope sprouting bristles.

"Oh, for heaven's sake," Juliana answered, starting in that direction. Normally, she was not easily exasperated, but the day had been a long and eventful one, and it wasn't over.

Lincoln leaned in his chair, caught hold of her hand and stopped her. Rising, he said, "I'll do it. Brew yourself up a cup of tea. Ma likes the stuff, and there's a tin of it around here somewhere."

Juliana sank into a chair.

"Bill," Lincoln said, approaching the pantry door. "Quit fooling around, now. It's time to scrub you down a layer."

Billy-Moses appeared in the pantry doorway, still looking petulant. "*Joseph* didn't have to take a bath," he protested.

"Reckon he'll get around to it tomorrow sometime," Lincoln said easily. Then he bent, hooked Billy-Moses around the waist with one bent arm and carried him through the kitchen.

Billy-Moses squealed with a little boy's joy, kicking and squirming, and it was a sound Juliana had never heard him make before.

As soon as she was alone, Juliana folded her arms on the tabletop and rested her head on them.

Mr. Philbert would come, and soon. She could almost feel him bearing down on Stillwater Springs, on her, full of righteous wrath. How would she explain to Billy-Moses, only four, and Daisy, just three, that he would be taking them far away, handing them over to strangers? Would he even give her a *chance* to explain?

She stood slowly, crossed to the sink and pumped water into the teakettle, found the tin Lincoln had mentioned earlier and a yellow crockery pot. By the time the brew was ready, he'd returned to the kitchen, grinning, his shirtfront soaked with water.

"Bill's been bedded down," he said. "I've wrestled yearling calves with less fight in them."

Juliana smiled. Here, then, was the reason Billy-Moses

hadn't asked Gracie to spell out his whole name with her alphabet blocks earlier that evening; he'd wanted "Bill." Because that was what Lincoln called him.

"Thank you," she said, warming her hands around her cup of tea.

Lincoln poured lukewarm coffee for himself, drew back his chair and sat down. With a slight nod of his head, he answered, "You're welcome, Mrs. Creed."

Once again, the name soothed her, and conversely that very fact made her uneasy. "Do you think the reverend will be warm enough in the barn?"

"He's bunking in between two bearskins, Juliana, and the animals put out a lot of body heat. The barn's warmer than the house a lot of the time."

Body heat. What an intriguing—and disturbing—term. She looked away, her tea forgotten.

And that was when Lincoln's hand, calloused by years of ranch work, came to rest on hers. "Maybe you ought to turn in for the night," he suggested.

She swallowed, nodded. Could not pull her hand out from under his, even—*especially*—when he began to stroke the backs of her knuckles with the rough pad of his thumb, setting her on fire inside.

Was this passion, this ache he aroused in her with the simplest touch of his hand?

Juliana was not prepared to find out.

"I'll be along in a while," Lincoln told her.

She stood.

He stood, too.

"Juliana?"

She met his gaze.

"Don't be afraid," he said.

How *not* to be afraid? She'd never experienced anything more daring than John's hand-patting and chaste pecks on the cheek during their brief and bland engagement.

She nodded and turned to leave.

LINCOLN HAD LOST INTEREST in the newspaper. The *Stillwater Springs Courier* came out once a week, if Wes got around to writing the articles and setting the type. As often as not, he didn't—but he was a good writer when he had something to say, and Lincoln usually enjoyed his brother's sly but often lethal wit. Hell, even some of the obituaries were funny, and the opinion pieces kept things stirred up around town.

With a sigh, Lincoln pushed the paper away and rose

from his chair. He carried his cup and Juliana's to the sink and left them there, stood with his hands braced against the counter, staring out the window, looking past his own reflection and into the darkness.

Flakes of snow drifted down, and he wondered if they'd stick or melt away by morning.

He felt restless. He knew he wasn't tired enough to lie down beside Juliana and keep his hands to himself. He'd wanted a wife—someone to share his bed, bear him more children, provide the motherly affection Gracie craved—but not one who touched his heart. No, he had not planned on that part.

Resigned, he went to the door, took his hat and coat from their pegs and put them on. Quietly left the house.

He moved past the privy, past the Gainers' cabin, past the bunkhouse. The night air was cold, sweeping inside him somehow, scouring like a bitter wind.

He needed no lantern; even with the moon disappearing behind the clouds, enough light came through to illuminate the snow. Besides, he'd lived on this ranch all his life; he could have found any part of it with his eyes closed.

He reached the orchard—years ago, when they were

boys, he and Micah and Wes and Dawson had helped to plant those apple and pear trees—then made his way, sure-footed, over ground he knew as well as the back of his own right hand.

Beyond the orchard was the little cluster of gravestones and markers where his father, his brother, the two lost babies—and Beth—were buried.

He didn't pause beside Josiah Creed's grave, walked right past Dawson's, too, even though he'd loved his brother.

Beth's resting place was marked with a stone angel, now cloaked in snow.

Lincoln brushed off the shoulders and the wings with one hand. He crouched, ran his right forearm across his face. How many times had he come here, said goodbye to Beth? Sooner or later, there always seemed to be something more that wanted saying.

And she wasn't even here.

Gracie believed her mother was in heaven.

Lincoln flat didn't know where dead people went, or if they went anywhere at all. Most likely, though, the journey ended in a pine box under six feet of dirt, but of course he wouldn't have said that to Gracie.

Graves weren't really for the folks who'd passed on, he

supposed. They gave the ones left behind a place to go and remember, that was all.

"I got married today," he said, feeling foolish, but needing to say the words all the same. They came out sounding gruff. "Her name is Juliana, and Gracie—Gracie wants to call her Mama."

A raspy chuckle escaped Lincoln then. If that grave had been some kind of passageway between this world and the next, Beth would have clawed her way right up out of it and given him what-for.

"I loved you," he went on, sober again. "I probably always will. But I've been too lonesome, Beth, and so has Gracie. I need somebody to wake up beside, somebody waiting when I come in off the range after a long day. I want Gracie to have a woman to look to so she doesn't grow up to smoke cigars like Ma says she will. I know you can't hear me, and wouldn't like what I've got to say if you could, but I still had to say it."

As he stood again, Lincoln wondered what he'd expected—an answer? Beth's ghost, absolving him of his promise to leave his heart buried with her?

The snap of a branch in the nearby orchard alerted him that someone was approaching—as it had probably been meant to do. He almost expected a specter, though he knew who had tracked him even before he saw Tom moving across the snowy ground toward him. If that old Indian hadn't wanted him to hear, he wouldn't have.

Lincoln waited, without speaking, as his friend drew nearer.

"She's not here, Lincoln," Tom said. "Beth is not here."

"Don't you think I know that?" Lincoln demanded, rubbing the back of his neck with one hand. "Where *is* she, Tom? With the Great Spirit? Or down in that hole in the ground?"

"Why are you doing this to yourself?" Tom asked reasonably. "Coming out here in the dark and the cold when you've got a pretty bride waiting back at the house? Is it because you didn't count on *feeling* anything for Juliana?"

"I think Juliana is beautiful," Lincoln said tersely. "I think she's smart and brave, and I want her. But that's *all* I feel, Tom. I loved my wife."

"Your wife is dead."

"So I hear."

Tight-jawed, eyes flashing, Tom reached out with a palm and shoved hard at Lincoln's chest, so he had to scramble to keep his footing. "Let Beth go," he almost growled. "Juliana doesn't deserve to go through what your mother did."

"What the hell is *that* supposed to mean?"

"It *means,* you damn fool, that your pa married your mother for pretty much the same reasons you married Juliana. He and Micah were alone after his first wife died, and he wanted to give the boy a mother. He never loved Cora, always mooning over his poor lost Mary, and your ma's life was a misery because of it."

Lincoln's mouth dropped open. He took a second or two to get his jaw hinged right so it would shut again. It was the first he'd heard of any of this, and that chafed at something raw inside him. It also explained why Cora couldn't keep the names of Micah's four sons straight, why she never visited them in Colorado or even wrote them letters. Maybe it even explained why Micah had lit out for another state the way he had and never looked back, as far as Lincoln could tell.

"Why tell me this now?" he asked bitterly, but his mind was still reeling, still scrabbling for some kind of purchase. Micah was his father's son, but not his mother's? In that moment, he understood what folks meant when they said they'd had the rug pulled out from under them.

"Because you need to know it."

"I would have appreciated somebody's mentioning this before Micah left home for good," Lincoln said, fighting down the old hurt. "I looked up to him. I didn't even get to say goodbye. One day, he was just—gone."

"Micah didn't leave because things weren't good between him and Cora. He left because he'd always had leaving in him."

"And because his mother's folks lived in Colorado," Lincoln guessed.

"Yes," Tom said.

Lincoln thrust out a sigh, felt a letting-go inside him. "Well, I don't have to wonder what I did wrong anymore, I guess. Does Wes know all this?"

A nod. "He knows."

"Am I the only one who didn't?"

"Let it go, Lincoln. Wes is a little older. He overheard more, that's all."

"I suppose now you're going to tell me my ma was so lonesome, you had to comfort her, and I'm *your* son, not Josiah Creed's." For a brief moment, Lincoln held his breath, hoping it was true.

Tom clenched a fist, looked as though he might throw

a punch. "If you were my son," he said, through his teeth, "I'd have claimed you a long time ago. No woman ever loved a man more than your ma loved Josiah Creed. She bore him three healthy boys and raised the one he brought with him when they married. When Dawson was killed, Josiah told her it was her fault, because it was one of her kin that pulled the trigger. To the day he died, he never had a kind word for her."

Lincoln closed his eyes for a long moment, let out the breath he hadn't realized he'd been holding. "But *you* loved my mother all these years, didn't you, Tom? That's why you stayed."

"I stayed because that's what I chose to do," Tom said coldly.

Lincoln started back toward the house, and Tom fell into step beside him.

They walked in silence with nothing more to say.

THERESA, BILLY-MOSES AND DAISY were sound asleep in Mrs. Creed's bed. Careful not to wake them, Juliana tucked the blankets in close and added wood to the fire in the stove.

She looked in on Gracie next, found her sleeping, too. Felt her heart seize with love for this child, the fruit of another woman's womb. It was a dangerous thing, caring so much, but it was too late. Just as it was with Daisy and Billy-Moses, Theresa and Joseph.

Juliana adjusted Gracie's covers and tiptoed out into the corridor.

In Lincoln's room, she lit a lamp. Slowly undressed, took her own nightgown from her satchel and put it on. After drawing a deep breath, she pulled back the covers and climbed into bed.

There, she waited.

Lincoln had promised to wait until she felt ready to give herself to him. That should have lessened her fears, but it didn't, because it wasn't the prospect of his love-making that frightened her most. It was her own desire to give herself up to him with total abandon.

He came in quietly, with the smell of the outdoors on his clothes—snow, pine, fresh, cold air. Feigning sleep, she watched through her eyelashes as he lowered one suspender, then the other.

"I know you're awake," he told her. "Most folks don't hold their breath when they're sleeping."

Juliana huffed out a sigh and opened her eyes.

After looking down at her for a long moment, he

chuckled and reached to extinguish the lamp. "Move over, Mrs. Creed," he said. "I'm going to need more than an inch of that mattress."

Juliana scooted closer to the wall, her heart pounding. Lincoln was not going to force himself on her, she knew that if little else. He wouldn't touch her in any intimate way without her permission.

She ought to relax.

But she couldn't. What did married people say to each other at night when they got into bed?

He continued to undress. Dear God, did the man sleep naked? He didn't seem the sort to don a nightshirt.

She tried to take her thoughts in hand, but they wouldn't be governed. Instead, they scattered in every direction like startled chickens, squawking and flapping their wings.

Sure enough, she felt the bareness of his flesh, the hard warmth with its aura of chill.

He gave a long sigh. "Good night, Juliana," he said.

They both lay sleepless in the dark for a long time, neither one speaking, careful not to brush against each other.

Juliana should have been relieved.

Instead, she bit her lower lip hard, and hoped he wouldn't hear her crying.

Chapter Seven

Lincoln was on the range the next morning, having bid the Reverend Dettly farewell, his muscles aching from a long night of self-restraint, wanting Juliana and not taking her, when Wes rode up, looking as rumpled and dissolute as ever. The cattle had been fed and Lincoln was there alone, he and his horse, just looking at the herd and wondering if those critters were worth all the grief they caused him.

"Came to get my mule," Wes said. "Tom told me you were out here."

There were bulging bundles tied where his saddlebags should have been. Gifts for Gracie and the other children, no doubt—Wes and Kate were always generous at Christmas and on birthdays, having no kids of their own.

Lincoln didn't say anything. Wes had known all along about Josiah's first wife, Micah's mother, and he'd never bothered to raise the subject. Now, after talking to Tom, he probably meant to make some kind of speech.

"A wire came for Miss Mitchell," Wes said, surprising him. "I thought I'd better bring it out here."

"She's not 'Miss Mitchell' anymore," Lincoln said, his tone flat and matter-of-fact. "I married her yesterday."

Wes gave a bark of pleased laughter at the news. "So *that's* why I met the reverend on the road out from town this morning," he said. "Congratulations, you lucky son of a gun."

"Thanks." He gave the word a grudging note.

Wes pulled a yellow envelope from the inside pocket of his coat, squinting against the glare of sunshine on snow. Watched as Lincoln tucked away the telegram without looking at the face of it.

"It's from the Bureau of Indian Affairs, Lincoln," Wes said quietly.

Trouble, of course—telegrams rarely brought good news. Lincoln swallowed and braced himself for whatever was coming. He'd been enduring things for so long, toughing them out, that he'd learned to dig in whenever a problem appeared. "You'd damn well better not have read it," he said.

"I didn't have to," Wes answered easily. "The telegraph operator told me what it says. By now, half the town knows that that Indian Agent Philbert means to show up in Stillwater Springs some time before New Year's and stir up a ruckus. The new Mrs. Creed is out of a job for sure, but I don't suppose that matters now, anyhow, what with the wedding and all."

Even though he'd expected something like that, the knowledge buffeted Lincoln like a hard wind. Made him shift in the saddle. "What else?" he asked, still avoiding his brother's gaze.

"He's bound on taking the kids back to Missoula," Wes said.

Lincoln closed his eyes. Didn't speak.

He'd get Joseph and Theresa on their way back to North Dakota before Philbert showed up, no matter what he had to do. Take them to the train depot at Missoula if it came to that, and put them onboard himself. Juliana had prepared herself for that particular parting—it was best for them to be with their own folks—but things were different with the two little ones. Orphans, the both of them. Somewhere along the line, Juliana had taken to mothering Daisy and little Bill, and letting go would be a hard thing, for her and for them.

"Tom told you the family secret, I hear," Wes said, when Lincoln had been silent too long to suit him.

Lincoln turned his head then. Looked straight at his brother. "Why didn't *you* tell me, Wes?"

"Ma asked me not to," Wes replied with the solemnity of truth.

Still, Lincoln had to challenge him. "Since when are you so all-fired concerned with doing what Ma wants?"

Wes's smile was thin, and a little on the self-disparaging side. "I chopped down a Christmas tree and hauled it out here on a mule's back because she told me to, didn't I?"

"You did that for Gracie."

Wes sighed, stood in the stirrups for a moment, stretching his legs. "Mostly," he admitted gruffly. Then, after a long time, he added, "Things weren't always so sour between Ma and me, Lincoln. You remember how it was after Dawson died—she was half-mad with the sorrow. Doc Chaney had to dose her up with laudanum. I was pretty torn up myself—we all were—but I felt sorry for her. I wanted to do what I could to help, and God knew there wasn't much."

Lincoln took that in without speaking. He remembered how his ma used to howl with grief some nights, during those first weeks after the shooting, and how his pa had slammed out of the house when she did.

Saddle leather creaked as Wes fidgeted, leaning forward a little, looking earnest. "There was another reason I didn't tell you," he said, sounding reluctant and a little irritated.

"What was that?" Lincoln bit out, in no frame of mind to make things easy for his brother. Whatever Wes's reasons for keeping that secret, he, Lincoln, had had as much right to know as anybody.

"You tend to hold on to things you ought to let go of," Wes said, reining his horse around, toward the main house, looking back at Lincoln over one shoulder. "People, too."

"Beth." Lincoln sighed the name.

"Beth," Wes agreed. Another silence fell between them, lengthy and punctuated only by snorts and hoof-shuffling from their horses and the chatter of the passing creek. "Of the four of us, Lincoln, you're the most like Pa. Tougher than hell, and too smart for your own good or anybody else's. You've held on to this ground, just like he did, and made it pay, in good times and bad. But you take after the old man in a few other ways, too. If I hauled off and swung a shovel at your head—and I've wanted to more than once—it would be the shovel that fractured, not your skull."

"That was quite a sermon, Wes."

"Don't get out of your pew yet, because I'm not finished. Right now, because you're still young, that stubborn streak serves you pretty well—you probably think of it as 'determination.' Trouble is, over time, it might just harden into something a lot less admirable."

As much as Lincoln would have liked to disregard the warning, he couldn't. It made too much sense. He'd mourned Dawson in a normal way, but since Beth had died, he'd boarded over parts of himself, knowing it would hurt too much if he let himself care.

"What do you suggest I do?" he asked moderately, just to get it over with. Wes was going to tell him anyhow; he'd worked himself up into a pretty good lather since talking with Tom.

"You remember how different Pa was when we were little? How he'd haul one or another of us around on his shoulders, let us follow him practically every place he went? How he laughed all the time, even though he worked like a mule? Back then, he wouldn't have believed it if somebody had told him he'd wind up turning his back on all of us, but he did. You know why, Lincoln? Because he decided to go right on loving a dead woman, when he had a living, breathing one right in front of him. It took a while, but that decision—that one bone-headed decision—poisoned his mind, and eventually, it poisoned his soul, too." Wes paused for a few moments, remembering, maybe gathering more words. "Never mind Juliana. She's prettier than Ma was, and she's got a lot more spirit. She'll be all right, even if you're fool enough to keep your heart closed to her. But what about Gracie? She's already got a mind of her own, and she's only seven—what do you think she'll be like at sixteen? Or eighteen? She'll make a lot of choices along the way, and I guarantee you aren't going to like some of them. You're bound to butt heads—I suppose that's normal—but if you aren't careful, you might find yourself treating your daughter the same way Pa did us. Do you want that?"

Lincoln's throat had seized shut. He shook his head.

Wes had finally run down, having reeled out what he had to say. He nudged at his horse's sides with the heels of his boots and rode back toward the house to drop off the things stuffed into those bags tied behind his saddle and collect his mule.

Conscious of the telegram in his pocket, Lincoln waited awhile before following.

JULIANA WAS CROSSING THE YARD, returning from a brief visit to Rose-of-Sharon and baby Joshua, when she saw her brother-in-law leading his mule out of the barn. Tom, meanwhile, carried two burlap bags, stuffed full of something, toward the woodshed.

Because she liked Weston Creed, she changed course, smiling, and went to greet him.

His smile flashed, but his eyes were solemn, almost sad. "My brother," he said, "is a lucky man."

Juliana blushed. She wasn't used to compliments; schoolmarms didn't get a whole lot of them. "We've got two big turkeys for Christmas dinner," she told him, feeling self-conscious. "I hope you'll join us."

He slipped a loop of rope around the mule's neck and

paused to look toward the house. "Is Kate welcome, too?" he asked. Without waiting for an answer, he moved to stand beside his horse and tied the other end of the rope loosely around the horn of the saddle.

"Of course," Juliana said.

"Do you know anything about her?" Weston asked, and while the inquiry sounded almost idle, Juliana knew it wasn't.

"I suppose she's your wife."

He chuckled, but it was a bitter sound, void of amusement. "Something like that," he said. "Kate owns the Diamond Buckle Saloon. She and I have been living in sin for some time now."

"Oh," Juliana said. She was intrigued at the prospect of meeting such a colorful personage, but perhaps she should have spoken to Lincoln before she'd issued the invitation.

"Yes," Weston said wryly. "Oh."

Juliana's cheeks stung with embarrassment. When she'd asked Lincoln for permission to bathe Daisy and Billy-Moses the night before, he'd said the ranch house was her home, too, and she didn't need his permission. She hoped that liberty extended to other things. "We'll sit down to dinner around two o'clock," she said. Since she wouldn't be roasting the turkeys, the hour was a mere guess. "But whatever time you and Kate arrive, we'll be glad to see you."

He rounded the horse to stand facing Juliana. His mouth, sensuous like Lincoln's, twitched at one corner. "You do realize, Mrs. Creed, that the roof will surely fall in, either the instant Kate sets foot over the threshold or when my mother finds out?"

Even without meeting the woman, Juliana was a little afraid of Cora Creed. Just the same, she wasn't one to let fear stop her from doing anything she thought was right. Raising her chin a notch, she replied, "I guess we'll have to take that chance."

Lincoln's brother chuckled again, but this time, it sounded real. "Brave words," he said. "But I think you might just mean them."

"I never say anything I don't mean, Mr. Creed."

"Call me Wes," he said, grinning now.

"Only if you agree to call me Juliana," she retorted.

He leaned in, kissed her forehead. "Welcome to my brother's life, Juliana," he told her. "God knows, he needs you."

Something made her look up then. She saw Lincoln approaching on horseback, a distant speck, moving slowly. Her heart quickened at the sight. "What makes you say that?" she asked Wes.

Wes sighed, and after glancing back over one shoulder, favored her with a sad smile. "He's lost a lot in his life. Beth, of course, and two babies. Pa and our brother Dawson. He's a good man, Lincoln is, but he's—well, he's mighty careful with his heart, as a general rule."

Juliana laid a hand to her chest; she had been too careful with her own heart, until Daisy and Billy-Moses and other special students had somehow gotten past the barriers.

Wes turned, stuck a foot in one stirrup and mounted the horse. After glancing in Lincoln's direction once more, he said, "I'll be going now. We've had a few words, my brother and I, and there will be more if I stay." He tapped at his horse's sides with the heels of his boots, tightened the rope to urge the mule into motion. "Unless there's another blizzard," he added, "Kate and I will be here Christmas Day."

Juliana smiled, though she was a little troubled by talk of he and Lincoln "having words." "Come early," she said.

Wes nodded and started off, the mule balking at first, then trotting obediently along behind his horse.

Although it was sunny out, the weather was cold.

Juliana huddled inside one of her mother-in-law's cloaks, hastily borrowed, and waited for her husband.

When he rode up to the barn, she approached, slowly at first, and then with faster steps.

The confession burst out of her. "I've asked Wes and Kate to come for Christmas dinner," she said, all on one breath.

He swung down from the saddle, stood looking at her with amusement on his mouth and sadness in his eyes, just as Wes had done. "Did he accept the invite?" he asked.

She took a breath, let it out and nodded quickly.

He laughed then, and hooked one stirrup over the saddle horn, so he could unbuckle the cinch. "Well, Mrs. Creed," he said, "you've succeeded where I failed, then. I've never been able to persuade Kate to set foot on this ranch, let alone sit down to Christmas dinner, and if she stays in town, so does Wes."

Juliana took a single step toward him, stopped herself, reading the set of his face. "Something is wrong," she said. "What is it?"

He went still for a long moment, then reached into his coat pocket and brought out a small yellow envelope.

Seeing it, Juliana felt her blood run cold. She was suddenly paralyzed.

Lincoln held out the envelope to her, and her hands trembled as she accepted it. Fumbled as she tried to unseal the flap.

"Wes brought it out from town," Lincoln said.

Juliana began to shiver, finally shoving the telegram at Lincoln. "Please," she whispered. "Read it."

Lincoln tugged off his gloves, opened the envelope and studied the page inside. "It's from the Bureau of Indian Affairs," he said. From his tone, it was clear that he'd known that all along. "'Miss Mitchell. You are hereby—'" Lincoln paused, cleared his throat. "'You are hereby dismissed. I will be in Stillwater Springs by the first of January at the latest. At that time, you will surrender any remaining students now in your custody for placement in appropriate institutions.' It's signed 'R. Philbert.'"

Juliana stood absolutely still, though on the inside, she felt as though she were set to bolt in a dozen different directions.

Lincoln took hold of her shoulders, the telegram still in one hand, and steadied her. "Take a breath, Juliana," he ordered, his voice low.

She breathed. Once. Twice. A third time.

"Listen to me," Lincoln went on calmly. "We're going to handle this, you and I. Together."

Juliana's mind raced, but there was a painful clarity to her thoughts just the same. Mr. Philbert had effectively warned her by sending her a telegram announcing his intention to visit Stillwater Springs, which might mean he planned to come earlier, hoping to forestall any attempt she might make to flee with the children.

"Wh-what are we going to do?" she faltered.

"First, we've got to get Joseph and Theresa to Missoula, put them on a train east. As for Daisy and Bill—well—I've been thinking about what Gracie said yesterday. Now that we're married, we could adopt them, and then they'd be Creeds. They could stay with us."

Juliana was grateful for his hold on her shoulders, because her knees wanted to buckle. "You'd do that?" she whispered, marveling. Surely there wasn't another man on the face of the earth quite like this one.

His eyes were shadowed by the brim of his hat, but she saw a quiet willingness in them even before he answered. "Yes."

"Why?"

"For them. For Gracie. Most of all, for you." Gently,

he turned her toward the house. Spoke close to her right ear, his breath warm against her skin. "Go on inside before you catch your death in this cold. I'll be in as soon as I get this horse put up."

Juliana took a cautious step, found that her legs were still working.

Inside, the children, having finished the day's lessons, were pestering Tom to let them go out to play. Juliana gave her permission, with the stipulation that they must all bundle up as warmly as possible and not make noise near the Gainers' cabin because Rose-of-Sharon and the baby needed peace and quiet.

There was a flurry of coat-finding—Gracie was so excited, she could hardly stand still to let Juliana lay a woolen scarf over the top of her head and tie it beneath her chin. Tom found knitted caps for the other children, and they all raced for the front door.

Once they were gone, Tom asked straight out, "You're pale as a new snow, Juliana. What's the matter? What's happened?"

Haltingly, she told him about Mr. Philbert's telegram.

His face hardened as he listened. "What did Lincoln have to say about that?"

"He wants to get Joseph and Theresa to the train in Missoula as soon as possible." She didn't mention the adoption; she still wasn't sure she'd actually heard Lincoln correctly, where that was concerned.

Tom nodded. "Missoula's half a day's ride from here, if the weather holds," he said. "If it doesn't, Philbert probably won't make it to town until the roads are clear."

Lincoln came in just then, looked from Juliana to Tom without speaking, took off his hat and coat and hung them up the way he always did. His expression remained grim.

"I'll take Joseph and Theresa to Missoula," Tom said. "Ride back to North Dakota with them to make sure they get there all right and folks are ready to take them in on the other end."

Sadness moved in Lincoln's face, but he nodded. Looking distracted, he said, "I'll be at my desk." Pausing in the doorway to the front room, he turned around. "You'll come back, won't you, Tom?" he asked.

Tom didn't smile. "I'll come back," he said very quietly.

Later, when the children had worn themselves out playing games in the front yard and returned to the house, bright-eyed and glowing from the cold, Juliana brewed up a batch of hot chocolate in a heavy cast-iron kettle and gave them each a cup. While they enjoyed the treat, she went in search of Lincoln.

He was where he'd said he'd be, seated at his desk in a corner of the front room, surrounded by thick books, all of them open. As she approached, he dipped a pen in a bottle of ink and wrote something on a sheet of paper.

Needing to be near him, she set a mug of hot chocolate beside him. "Thanks," he said.

Juliana's fingers flexed; she wanted to work the tight muscles in Lincoln's neck and shoulders, but refrained. Yes, he was her husband, but touching him, even in such an innocuous way, seemed too familiar. Even a little brazen.

Still, she could not bring herself to walk away, any more than she could have left a warm stove after walking through a blizzard.

"If you're going to linger, Juliana," he said mildly, without looking up from the paper and the books, "please sit down."

She moved to a nearby armchair, sat down on its edge, knotted her fingers together. And waited.

Lincoln finally sighed, shoved back his chair and turned to look at her. "Everything will be all right, Juliana," he said.

He didn't know Mr. Philbert. "Today," she ventured nervously, "out by the barn, I thought you said—"

He waited.

"I thought you said you would be willing to adopt Daisy and Billy-Moses."

Lincoln smiled. "I did say that, Juliana."

She gripped the arms of her chair. "How?"

"I'm a lawyer," he answered. He gestured toward the books on his desk. "I'm drawing up the papers right now."

"You didn't mention that. Being a lawyer, I mean."

"There are a lot of things I haven't gotten around to mentioning," Lincoln said reasonably. "I haven't had time."

She stood up, sat down again. "You could—you could get into trouble for sending Joseph and Theresa to North Dakota," she fretted.

"I'm no stranger to trouble," Lincoln told her. "In fact, I like a challenge."

"I need something to do," she confessed.

Lincoln opened a drawer in his desk, brought out a second bottle of ink and a pen. Gave her several sheets of paper. "Write to your brother," he said. "Tell him you're married now, and if he doesn't come here first, I'll be paying him a visit one day soon."

The thought of Clay and Lincoln standing face-to-face unnerved her a little, but she accepted the pen and ink and paper, and went back to the kitchen. Tom and Joseph were gone, and Theresa, Gracie, Daisy and Billy-Moses sat in a circle on the floor, playing with a tattered deck of cards.

She took a chair at the table, opened the ink bottle and awaited inspiration. After a quarter of an hour, all she'd written was "Dear Clay." Finally, out of frustration, she stopped trying to choose her words carefully, dipped the pen, and began.

As you have long wished me safely married, I am happy to inform you that yesterday, December 22, I entered into matrimony with Mr. Lincoln Creed, of Stillwater Springs, Montana—

Juliana went on to describe Lincoln, Gracie, the house and what she'd seen of the ranch. She extended sincere felicitations for a happy Christmas and prosperous New Year. Why, it would be 1911 soon. Where had the time gone?

The letter filled three pages by the time she'd finished.

She closed with "Sincerely, Juliana Mitchell Creed," and when the ink was dry, she carefully folded the letter, her earlier trepidation having given way to relief. She could not predict how Clay would respond to the missive, if he responded at all, but that took nothing away from her sense of having turned some kind of corner, found some new kind of freedom.

The rest of the day ground by slowly.

The younger children took naps without protest.

Theresa read quietly in the rocking chair, next to the stove.

When she grew restless, Juliana avoided the front room, where Lincoln was still working, and donned the borrowed cloak and went to the Gainers' cabin again, knocking lightly on the door. When Ben answered, whispering that Rose-of-Sharon and the baby were asleep, she smiled to cover her disappointment and promised to come back later.

She visited the barn and spoke to the cow and all the horses.

She went into the woodshed, planning to peek into the two burlap bags Tom had left there, but the idea pricked at her conscience, so she dismissed it.

She was chilled, but too wrought up to return to the house.

Spotting the orchard nearby, Juliana headed in that direction. The trees were gnarled and bare-limbed, and she paused, laid a hand to a sturdy trunk. Late the following summer, there would be fruit. In the meantime, perhaps Tom would teach her to make preserves.

At first, glimpsing the stone angel out of the corner of her eye, Juliana thought she was seeing things. As she drew nearer, though, she realized she'd come upon a small cemetery.

The angel marked the final resting place of Bethany Allan Creed.

Juliana's throat tightened. Beth. Lincoln's first wife, Gracie's mother. Careful of her skirts—she was wearing the blue dress again—she dropped to her haunches. Brushed away a patch of snow, and the twigs and small stones beneath.

She couldn't have said why she felt compelled to do such a thing. "I'm going to take very good care of your little Gracie," she heard herself say. "She's so smart, and so pretty and so kind. I fell in love with her right away."

A breeze, neither warm nor cold, played in Juliana's hair. "I'll make you a promise, Beth, here and now. Gracie won't forget you, won't forget that you're her real mother."

Behind her, a twig snapped.

Startled, Juliana stood and, forgetting to lift her hem, spun around.

Lincoln stood at the edge of the orchard, wearing his round-brimmed hat and his long black coat. From that distance, she couldn't read his expression.

Feeling as though she'd been caught doing something wrong, Juliana didn't move or speak.

Lincoln came toward her slowly. Even when she could see his face clearly, she found no emotion there. No anger, but no smile, either.

"There are wolves out here sometimes, Juliana," he said. "In the summer, the bears like to raid the orchard. It isn't safe to wander too far from the house alone."

Juliana fought to speak, because her throat was still closed. "You must have loved your wife very much," she said, brushing the angel's wing with a light pass of her hand.

"Beth's father sent the marker," he said. "Nothing but the best for his daughter. Not that he bothered to come all the way out here to the wilds of Montana to pay his respects or meet his granddaughter."

Juliana didn't know what to say. And she probably couldn't have spoken, anyway. Despite Lincoln's lack of expression, the air felt charged with emotion.

"I did love Beth," he continued, when she held her tongue. "The strange thing is, if I met her today, for the first time, I mean, I'm not sure I'd do more than tip my hat."

Juliana reached out without thinking and touched his arm. Was relieved when he didn't pull away. "What do you mean?" she asked softly.

"I was a different man back then," he answered.

Although she was still puzzled, Juliana didn't ask for clarification. Instinct told her to listen instead.

"I wanted different things than I want now."

Juliana waited, her hand still resting on the sleeve of his coat.

He was quiet for a long time. When he broke the silence, his voice sounded hoarse. He told her about his father, his mother, his three brothers. He told her about going off to college in Boston, how homesick he'd been for the ranch and his family, about studying law and meeting Beth when he went to work in her father's firm.

He told her about Gracie's birth, and the two babies who hadn't lived—a boy and a girl. They'd never given them names, and now he wished they had, because then they'd have had identities, however brief.

Juliana didn't look away, though she would have liked to hide the tear that slipped down her right cheek.

Finally, he reached out, took her hand. Led her toward home.

Tom had made supper—bear-meat hash—and Juliana was surprised to find that she had an appetite. Most likely, it was all that fresh air.

She washed the dishes by herself that night, while Theresa got the three younger children ready for bed. Tom and Lincoln sat at the table with Joseph, making plans for the journey to North Dakota.

Juliana listened, knowing that the ache of missing Joseph and Theresa would be with her for a long, long time. They belonged with their family, though—shouldn't have been taken from them in the first place.

She finished the dishes, hung the dish towel up to dry. Left the kitchen.

Gracie had climbed into bed with Daisy and Billy-Moses. Theresa sat cross-legged on the foot of the mattress, reading aloud from, of all things, the Sears, Roebuck catalog.

Juliana stood in the open doorway for a while, unnoticed, while the children listened raptly to descriptions of china platters, teacups and silverware. The words, she realized, didn't matter. It was the sound of another human voice that held their attention.

She slipped away. In Lincoln's room, she filled the china basin with fresh water from the matching pitcher and scrubbed her teeth with a brush and baking soda. She washed her face, unplaited her hair, brushed it thoroughly, and plaited it again.

Her nightgown felt chilly, so she draped it over the screen in front of the fireplace where a cheery blaze crackled. Lincoln must have lit the fire just before supper.

She unbuttoned the blue dress, stepped out of it. Took off her shoes and rolled her stockings down and off. Untied the laces of her petticoat and let the garment fall.

She was standing there, in just her camisole and bloomers, when the door opened and Lincoln came in.

He went still at the sight of her.

She imagined that the firelight behind her had turned her undergarments transparent, and that sent a rush of embarrassment through her, but she made no move to cover herself.

Lincoln started to back out of the room.

"Wait," Juliana said with dignity. "Don't go. Please."

He stepped over the threshold again, closed the door behind him. The conflict in his handsome face might have been comical, if she hadn't been so concerned with the pounding of her heart. He opened his mouth to speak, but when no sound came out, he closed it again.

"You asked me to tell you when I felt ready," she reminded him. Fingers trembling, she began untying the tiny ribbons that held her camisole together in front.

"And?" He rasped the word.

"I'm ready."

Chapter Eight

Leaning back against the bedroom door, Lincoln shook his head once and gave a raspy sigh. "I'm not so sure about that," he said. "Your being ready, I mean."

Was he rejecting her? Quickly, cheeks throbbing with heat, Juliana stopped untying the camisole ribbons and stood frozen in injured confusion. Without intending to, she allowed her deepest fear to escape. "Don't you—don't you want me, Lincoln?"

He blew out a breath. "Oh, I *want* you, all right," he said.

"Then, why…?"

"My brother said some things to me today that I need to think about," Lincoln explained calmly. "And, anyway, you've been through a lot lately. I won't have you doing this because you think you ought to, or because you want to get it over with."

"Get it over with?" She was astounded, but she probably sounded angry.

His powerful shoulders moved in a shruglike motion. "Making love can be painful for the woman the first time," he reminded her. "And it'll be more so, in a lot of other ways, if you're offering yourself to me for the wrong reasons."

He was such a—*lawyer,* building a case against what they both needed and wanted. "*What* wrong reasons?" she demanded, careful to keep her voice down, so none of the children would overhear. Earlier, he'd found her visiting his first wife's grave. Did he think she was trying to exert some kind of *claim* on him, somehow supplant Beth's memory? Use her body to push the other woman out of his heart and mind?

Lincoln raised one eyebrow. "Well," he began, "you could be grateful, because I'm willing to adopt Daisy and Bill and raise them as our own."

Indignant, Juliana snatched her nightgown off the fireplace screen and pulled it on over her head, meaning to remove her undergarments later, when he was gone. As luck would have it, though, she got her arms tangled in the sleeves somehow and ended up flailing about like a chicken inside a burlap sack.

Lincoln laughed; she heard him come toward her, his footsteps easy on the plank floor.

She felt him righting the nightgown.

When he tugged it down so her head popped through the neck hole, his eyes were dancing.

"Don't you *dare* make fun of me!" Juliana sputtered.

He chuckled again, but there was something tender in the way he held her shoulders. "I wouldn't do that," he said.

As if she weren't humiliated enough already, hot tears sprang to her eyes.

"Listen," Lincoln said, after placing a light kiss on the top of her head. "Once we've made love, there will be no going back. It's got to be right."

She stared at him, aghast. *Once we've made love, there will be no going back.* Was he having second thoughts, thinking of annulling the marriage on the grounds that they had yet to consummate it?

"May I remind you, Mr. Creed, that getting married was *your* idea?"

"I'm well aware of that," he said affably.

"But now you want to make sure there's a way to *go back?*"

Surprise widened his eyes. "Hell, *that* isn't what I meant," he said.

Relief swept over Juliana, leaving her almost faint. She hoped to high heaven her reaction didn't show, because she'd made enough of a fool of herself as it was, behaving with such wanton abandon. "I practically *threw myself* at you," she fretted, "and you might as well have flung a bucket of cold water all over me!"

He sighed, yet again. "Oh," he said.

"Oh," Juliana repeated, in the same tone Wes had used when he'd repeated the word back to her that afternoon, in reference to Kate's reasons for avoiding the ranch.

Lincoln shoved a hand through his hair. "Maybe we ought to just start over—"

"Maybe," Juliana shot back, "you should go off by yourself and *think* about whatever it was that your brother said to you, out there on the range."

Something flickered in his eyes. "I believe I've come

to terms with that," he said, and his voice sounded different. It was lower than before, and gruff in a way that made Juliana tingle in peculiar places. Her mouth went dry.

She waited for him to explain further, but, of course, he didn't, being a man and used to keeping his own counsel. He raised his hands to the sides of her face, the way he'd done after the marriage ceremony, and then he kissed her.

The wedding kiss had rocked her, but this one was even more intense. He parted her lips and used his tongue, and the pleasure of that was so startling that Juliana would have cried out if her mouth hadn't been covered.

She slipped her arms around his neck and rose onto her tiptoes, caught up in her response like a leaf swept up into a whirlwind.

His tongue.

The way his body fit against hers.

The way her own expanded, ready to take him in.

All of it left her dazed, and when he finally stopped kissing her, he had to grab her shoulders again, because she swayed.

Blinking, she stared up at him.

"*That,* Mrs. Creed, should settle any question of whether I want you or not."

It had certainly settled the question of whether or not *she* wanted *him*. She most definitely did, and the consequences be damned.

"Then you'll make love to me?" she asked, brazen, flushed with desire.

"Inevitably," he answered, but he was releasing her shoulders, turning to leave the room. Only her pride, or what remained of it, kept her from scrambling after him, begging him not to leave.

"When?" she croaked.

He paused without turning to face her, and tilted his head back, considering. "When it's right," he finally replied.

And then he was gone.

Juliana felt like some wild creature, caught and caged. She stood there trembling with rage and frustration for a few moments, then took up her brush, undid her braid and brushed her hair with long, furious strokes that left it crackling around her face like fire.

Once she'd regained her composure enough to risk leaving the room, she went to look in on the children. Billy-Moses, Daisy and Gracie lay curled against one another like puppies, sleeping soundly. Theresa was in Gracie's bed with her eyes closed.

Just as Juliana would have closed the door, though, the child spoke.

"Miss Mitchell—I mean, Mrs. Creed? Will you sit with me—just for a little while?"

Juliana approached the bed, sat down on its edge. Smoothed Theresa's dark hair with a motherly hand. "Sure," she said softly. "Is something bothering you?"

A stray moonbeam played over the girl's face, was gone again. "Joseph remembers the folks at home," she said. "I do, too, sort of, but mostly I remember going away and living in a lot of different schools."

Juliana simply waited.

"What if we get home, Joseph and me, and they can't keep us for some reason? Or don't want us after all?"

Juliana's heart ached. "You saw the letter they sent," she said gently. "They want you."

"But maybe somebody like Mr. Philbert will come and take us away again."

"I don't think that will happen," Juliana said. Although unlikely, it *was* possible. "Tom is going with you, remember. He'll make sure you and Joseph get settled, and keep you safe all along the way."

"Folks might be mean to us. After all, Mr. Dancingstar is an Indian, too."

That, too, was possible. Juliana wished she could make the trip with the three of them, and stand guard over them, but of course she couldn't. Gracie and Daisy and Billy-Moses needed her—if Wes Creed could be believed, so did Lincoln. She had to face Mr. Philbert and settle things, once and for all, so she and Lincoln could go on with their lives.

"Don't worry, Theresa," she said. "That won't change anything. And Mr. Dancingstar *will* take care of you."

"I almost wish I could stay here with you, but I'd miss Joseph something fierce, and he might forget to practice his reading if I don't keep an eye on him."

Juliana blinked back tears. "Will you write to me when you get home? Tell me all about the trip, and what things are like in North Dakota?"

Theresa nodded and reached up with both arms for a hug.

She and Juliana clung together for a little while.

"Will you write me back?" Theresa asked finally, settling back onto her pillow. "Long, long letters?"

"Long, long letters," Juliana promised, choking back

more tears. She leaned over, kissed the girl's smooth forehead. "Now, go to sleep, Theresa. Tomorrow is Christmas Eve."

"You don't think I believe all those stories about Saint Nicholas, do you?" Theresa asked in a whisper. "I'm twelve, you know. Besides, Joseph says it's all malarkey and I oughtn't to expect anything much."

With yet another pang, Juliana tucked the covers under Theresa's chin. "You mustn't stop hoping for things," she said. "Not ever. That's what keeps us all going."

"But Saint Nicholas *is* just a story?"

Juliana thought of the presents hidden in the top of Mrs. Creed's wardrobe. They were simple things, but seen through the eyes of these children, who'd never owned much of anything, they would gleam like Aladdin's treasure. "Yes," she admitted. "There was a real Saint Nicholas, once upon a time, and a lot of legends have grown up around his life, but they're just that, legends. Still, there *are* people in the world who have generous hearts."

Lincoln was one of them. Wes Creed was another. And, of course, Tom Dancingstar.

Theresa sighed, closed her eyes and settled into her dreams.

Juliana waited until she was sure the child was asleep, kissed her cheek and returned to the corridor.

She'd left the bedroom door open; now it was closed.

She stopped, put a hand to her throat before reaching to turn the knob.

The room was dark except for the flickering glow cast by the fireplace. Lincoln was already in bed, but sitting up with pillows behind his back. His chest was bare, she could tell, but his face was in shadow, making his expression impossible to read.

"I wondered if you'd come back to this room after our—discussion," he said.

"There is nowhere else to sleep," Juliana answered, and the formal tone she employed was at least partly an act. She wasn't angry with Lincoln, just confused. "Unless, of course, you'd prefer I retired to the barn like Reverend Dettly did."

Lincoln gave a snort. "The reverend is a man," he reminded her. "And despite being on a first-name basis with the Good Lord, he carries a gun in his saddlebags, right alongside his Bible."

Juliana folded her arms, keeping a stubborn distance from Lincoln Creed's bed, even though it was the very place she most wanted to be at that moment. "If you're going to be argumentative, perhaps *you* should sleep in the barn," she said, jutting out her chin. It was all bravado, and everything she said seemed to be coming out wrong—thinking one thing, saying quite another. What was the matter with her? "I was prepared to forgive you for your rudeness, Mr. Creed, but now I'm not so sure."

He chuckled, a low, rumbling sound, entirely masculine and not entirely polite. "That's very generous of you, *Mrs.* Creed," he answered. "Especially since I was trying to look out for your best interests, and if anybody ought to be apologizing around here, it's you."

"You were looking out for your own interests, not mine!" she whispered accusingly.

He patted the mattress. "Get into bed, Juliana. I'm tired and I won't be able to sleep with you standing there like you've got a ramrod stuck down the back of your nightgown."

Since her side of the bed was against the wall, she would have to crawl over him to get there, perhaps even straddling his limbs in the awkward effort. She wasn't *about* to do any such thing.

"Juliana," he repeated.

"The least you could do is get up and allow me to obey your *orders* with some semblance of dignity!"

He laughed then, though quietly. "You really want me to throw back the covers and stand up?" he teased. "Under the circumstances, that might be more than you bargained for."

Juliana reasoned that if she couldn't see Lincoln's face, he couldn't see *hers,* either, and that was a mercy, since she knew she was blushing again. It was the curse of redheaded women. "Oh, for heaven's sake!" she blurted, going to the side of the bed and scrambling over him, trying to keep her nightgown from riding up in the process.

Lincoln chortled at her predicament, and that made her want to pause long enough to pummel him with her fists. Once she'd crossed him, like some mountain range, she plopped down hard on her back and hugged her arms tightly across her chest, staring up at the ceiling.

He rolled onto his side, his face only inches from hers. "I'd like to propose a truce," he said. "I didn't mean to insult you, Juliana."

She didn't turn her head, but she did slant her eyes in his direction. "Do you apologize?"

Lincoln rose onto one elbow, cupping the side of his head in his palm. "Hell, no, I don't apologize. I didn't do anything wrong."

She turned away from him, onto her side.

He turned her back.

"All *right,*" he growled. "I'm sorry."

"You are not!"

That was when he kissed her again. She struggled at first, out of pure obstinacy, but he just kissed her harder and more deeply, and she melted, driven by instincts that came from some uncontrollable part of her being. Plunged her fingers into his hair and kissed him right back.

She felt his manhood pressed against her thigh as he shifted on the mattress, and the sheer size of it caused her eyes to pop open in alarm, but then that strange, weighted heat suffused her again. She sank into helpless wanting.

"God help me," he murmured, almost tearing his mouth from hers.

Juliana ran her hands up and down his back, loving the feel of hard, warm muscle under her palms.

Lincoln let his forehead rest against hers. "Woman," he said, "if you don't stop doing that, I won't be responsible for my actions."

She raised her head, nibbled at his bare shoulder and then the side of his neck.

With a groan, Lincoln shifted again, poised above her now, resting on his forearms to keep from crushing her. "Juliana," he ground out, but if he'd been planning to say more, the words died in his throat.

He kissed her tenderly this time, tugging at her lower lip, wringing a soft moan from her. Then, with one hand, he caught hold of her nightgown and hauled it upward, past her thighs, past her waist, past her breasts—and then over her head.

Casting the gown aside, Lincoln sat back on his haunches, the covers falling away behind him.

He moved to straddle her now, his knees on either side of her hips. Firelight danced over her skin, and he seemed spellbound as he looked at her.

When he took her breasts gently into his hands and chafed the nipples with the sides of his thumbs, Juliana was lost, already transported far beyond the borders of common sense.

She couldn't bear too much waiting, not this first time, when she was in such terrible, wonderful suspense, and he seemed to know that.

He deftly dispensed with her undergarments, parted her legs, and she felt that most intimate part of him, pressed against her.

"You're sure, Juliana?" he whispered.

She nodded.

He eased inside her, in a long, slow stroke, and there *was* pain, but the pleasure was so much greater, a fiery friction, inflaming her more with every motion of their bodies, blazing like a little sun at her core. She clutched at Lincoln, gasping, rising to meet him, and he soothed her with gruff murmurings even as he drove her mad.

She was straining for something, wild with the need of it, and then it was upon her, and at the same time, it was as though she'd somehow escaped herself, given herself up entirely to sensation.

Her body dissolved first, and then her mind, and then their very souls seemed to collide. Lincoln covered her mouth with his own, muffling both their cries.

When it was over—it seemed to go on for an eternity, that melting and melding of so much more than their bodies—Lincoln collapsed beside her, gathered her in his arms. Propped his chin on the top of her head.

After a long time, he asked hoarsely, "Did it hurt?"

"Yes," she told him honestly. Surely he'd been aware of her responses, of the pleasure he'd given her. She felt transformed, even powerful.

"I'm sorry."

Juliana turned onto her side, facing him. Touched his cheek. "Don't be sorry, Lincoln," she said. "It was the most *wonderful* thing."

He chuckled, kissed her lightly. "Now will you go to sleep?"

She laughed. Kissed him back. "Now I will go to sleep," she conceded.

With his arms still around her, Lincoln soon drifted off, his breathing deep and slow, his flesh warm. Perfectly content, Juliana lay there in the fire-lit darkness, marveling at all she had not known before this night.

AFTER THE CATTLE HAD BEEN FED the next morning—the weather remained mild, though Lincoln felt a rancher's wariness and made good use of it while he could—he rode to town.

At the mercantile, he mailed Juliana's letter to her brother and bought presents—a wedding band for his wife, along with several ready-made dresses and a bright green woolen cloak with a hood. He chose coats for the four children, too, guessing at their sizes, and because he'd so often seen Theresa reading, he added a thick book to the pile. There were other things, as well—a stick horse with a yarn mane for little Bill, a music box for Daisy, good pipe tobacco for Tom and a few things for the Gainers and their new baby.

While Fred Willand was wrapping it all in tissue paper, Lincoln crossed to the newspaper office, found it locked up and made for the Diamond Buckle Saloon.

Since it was early in the day, and Christmas Eve to boot, there were no customers. Kate, with her too-blond hair and low-cut dress, sat at one of the card tables, drinking coffee.

"Lincoln!" she said, beaming, starting to rise.

He motioned for her to stay in her chair, joined her at the table after placing a brotherly kiss on her rouged cheek. Like Wes, Kate was something worse for wear, a little tattered around the edges, but there was a remarkably pretty woman under all that paint and pretense.

"Is my brother around?"

Kate made a face. "He was up late, skinning honest working people out of their wages at five-card stud," she said. "Then he decided to write a piece for the paper on how the Bureau of Indian Affairs does more harm than good. Last time I saw him, he was under the blankets, snoring for all he was worth."

Lincoln chuckled at that. Wes had always been more alive at night—daylight was something he tended to wait out, like a case of the grippe—while Lincoln, a born rancher, wrung all the use he could from the hours between sunrise and sunset. "My new bride tells me you and Wes will be at the home place for Christmas Day," he said.

Kate looked worried now, as though he'd forced her into a corner and started poking at her with a cue stick from the rack next to the pool table. "Wes shouldn't have said we'd come," she said, her voice small and sad. She looked down at her gold satin dress, and the cleavage bulging above and behind her bodice. "I don't have anything proper to wear."

Lincoln reached out, took her hand. She wore a lot of cheap rings, and a row of bracelets that made a clinking sound whenever she moved her arm. "Juliana is going to be mighty disappointed if you don't come," he told her. "Gracie, too. It doesn't matter what you wear, Kate."

"What do you know? You're a man."

He sighed. "All right, then. There are trunks full of dresses out at the ranch, up in the attic. Take your pick."

"Beth's dresses," Kate scoffed, but there was hope in her hazel-colored eyes. "Lincoln, she was a little bitty thing and you know it. I'd never fit into anything she wore."

That, Lincoln thought, was probably true. "How about something of Ma's, then?" he suggested.

Wes appeared on the stairway just then, shirt untucked, feet bare, hair rumpled from sleep. He plunged his hands through it a lot when he was composing one of his hide-blistering opinion pieces for the *Courier.*

He scowled at Lincoln, even as Kate gave a throaty little chuckle. "Wouldn't *that* stick under the old lady's saddle like a spiky burr?" Lincoln remarked.

"What the devil are *you* doing here?" Wes grumbled at Lincoln, reaching the table, hauling back a chair next to Kate and falling into it as heavily as a sack of feed thrown from the back of a wagon. He winced when he landed, and closed his eyes for a moment, probably suffering his just deserts after a night passed drinking, gambling and puffing on cigars.

"I came to tell you that you were right about what you

said yesterday," Lincoln said, enjoying the visible impact this announcement had on Wes.

He opened his eyes, narrowed them suspiciously. Kate got up to head for the kitchen and fetch coffee for both of them. Lincoln could have done without, but Wes was plainly in dire need.

"Hold it," Wes ground out, grinning a little and working his right temple with the fingertips of one hand. "You just said I was *right*. Will you swear to it in front of witnesses?"

"Kate was a witness," Lincoln pointed out.

"I'm putting it on the front page. Two-inch headline. This is the biggest thing since McKinley's assassination, if not Honest Abe's."

Lincoln smiled, picked up a stray poker chip left behind after some previous game and turned it between his fingers. When he spoke, though, he looked serious, and he sounded that way, too. "I'm in love with Juliana, Wes," he confided. "And I'll be damned if I know how to tell her."

Wes leaned a little, laid a hand on Lincoln's shoulder, squeezed. "Same way you told Beth," he said quietly. "You just look her in the eye, open your mouth and say 'I love you.'"

Lincoln shifted uncomfortably in his chair, wishing

Kate would come back with that coffee, even though he didn't want it, so the conversation might turn in some easier direction.

"You *did* tell Beth you loved her, didn't you?" Wes challenged, looking worried.

"I thought she knew it," Lincoln confessed. "By the things I did, I mean."

"Keeping a roof over her head? Buying her geegaws and putting food on the table? Sweet Jesus, Lincoln, you're even more of a lunkhead than I thought you were."

Kate returned, a mug of steaming coffee in each hand and a big smile on her face—he'd struck home with that suggestion that she wear one of his ma's dresses to Christmas dinner, evidently—but her arrival didn't change the course of the conversation the way Lincoln had hoped it would.

She set a cup in front of each of them, and Wes scooted back his chair, caught hold of her hand and tugged hard so she landed, giggling like a girl, on his lap.

"I love you, Katie-did," he said.

"So you claim," Kate joked, blushing right down to the neckline of her faded dress. "But you've yet to put a gold band on my finger, Weston Creed."

He feigned surprise. "You'd actually hitch yourself to a waster like me?"

"You know I would," Kate said softly, looking and sounding wistful now.

"Then the next time the reverend comes through, we'll throw a wedding."

Lincoln, though pleased, wished he was elsewhere. The trouble with Wes was, he had no idea what was appropriate and what wasn't, but he seemed to be sincere enough, all things considered.

"Is that a promise?" Kate asked cautiously.

"It's a promise," Wes replied, setting her on her feet again, swatting her once on the bottom for emphasis. That done, he pivoted on his chair seat to look straight at Lincoln. "See, little brother? That's how you tell a woman you love her."

Lincoln merely shook his head. He reckoned Fred had the presents wrapped by then, and he was eager to get back out to the ranch. After all, Christmas was coming, and this one was special.

He stood. "You might want to ride out with me," he told his brother. "Kate's going to borrow one of Ma's dresses, and she'll need time to take it in a little first."

Wes gave a guffaw of laughter that made Kate jump and got to his feet. "That," he said, "will be worth seeing. But I'll meet you at the ranch later on—I've got to put on boots and get my horse saddled, and I don't want to hold you up."

"See you there," Lincoln agreed with a nod. He was halfway home, with his sack of presents tied behind his saddle, when Wes rode up alongside him.

They'd didn't speak of serious things—there had been enough of that and it was almost Christmas—except when they reached the barn. Lincoln unsaddled his horse, Wes didn't.

"Are you really going to marry Kate?" Lincoln asked, half-afraid of the answer. She'd be mighty let down if Wes's proposal turned out to be a joke, and by Lincoln's reckoning, Kate had had more than her share of disappointments as it was.

"Didn't I say that I would?"

"You say a lot of things, Wes."

"This time, I mean it."

Lincoln nodded. "I hope so," he replied, and that was the end of the exchange.

Inside the house, Wes was greeted with an armload of

Gracie, launching herself from the floor like a stone from a catapult, while the other kids hung back, looking stalwart and shy.

Wes noticed the way Juliana was glowing right away, and cast a sly look in Lincoln's direction before kissing her soundly on the forehead.

After that, the two brothers headed straight for their mother's bedroom and plundered the big mahogany wardrobe for a dress that would suit Kate without too much tucking and pinning. Flummoxed by the choices, they finally consulted Juliana, who chose a dusty-rose velvet day dress with a short jacket, pearl buttons and a nipped-in waist.

"Been a while since Ma could squeeze into *this,*" Wes observed, holding the getup against his front as if he meant to try it on himself.

"It will look fine on Kate," Lincoln said drily. "Personally, I think you'd look better in blue."

Juliana took the dress from Wes, carried it to the kitchen and proceeded to fold it neatly and wrap it up in leftover brown paper, tying the parcel closed with thick twine.

Gracie, having worked out that her beloved uncle and Kate were coming out to the ranch to share in tomorrow's celebration, issued an invitation of her very own. "Come *early,*" she pleaded, "because Papa probably won't let us see what Saint Nicholas brought until you get here."

Wes laughed, tugged at a lock of her hair. "Just what time is 'early'?" he asked. Of all the people in the world, Gracie was probably the only one he would have rolled out of the hay for. Lincoln had known him to sleep until four o'clock in the afternoon.

Gracie considered. "Six o'clock," she said.

Wes gave a comical groan.

"Uncle Wes," Gracie said firmly, "it's *Christmas.*"

"You could come out tonight," Lincoln suggested carefully. "Sleep in your old room."

Behind his grin, Wes went solemn, no doubt remembering how it had been when their father was still alive, and testy as an old bear with ear mites.

"Bed's wide enough for you and Kate," Lincoln added. "Since you and Micah used to share it."

"Maybe," Wes said thoughtfully.

"Say yes," Gracie ordered, hands resting on her hips.

"Maybe," Wes repeated. He glanced sidelong at Lincoln, an unspoken reminder of the warning he'd given out on the range the day before, probably. Gracie defi-

nitely *did* have a mind of her own, and as she grew up, she'd be a handful.

Nothing much was said after that. Wes took the gown, wrapped in its brown paper, and left.

Lincoln went to work on the adoption petition he'd been drafting, and Juliana visited the Gainers. The kids, having been given the day off from their lessons because it was Christmas Eve, chased one another all over the front yard until Juliana rounded them up on the way back from the cabin and brewed up another batch of hot cocoa.

For the rest of the day, Lincoln had half his mind on the petition and half on Juliana. The way she moved. The way she hummed under her breath and looked like she was all lit up from the inside.

Mentally, he rehearsed the words he wanted to say. *I love you.*

By sunset, the children were all so excited—except for Joseph, who showed a manful disdain for the proceedings—they could barely sit still to eat supper.

New snow drifted past the windows, and for once, Lincoln didn't dread it.

The dishes were done, the fires were stoked for a cold night.

The kids were all in bed, asleep. Or so they wanted him to believe.

Just as Lincoln was about to extinguish the lanterns and join Juliana in their bed—he'd been looking forward to that all day—he heard a rig roll up outside.

He grinned, put on his coat and hat. There would be a wagon to unhitch, a team to put up in the barn.

Juliana appeared, still wearing her day dress, just as he was opening the door to go outside.

"Wes and Kate are here," he said.

Juliana beamed, as happy at the prospect of company as any country woman would be. "I'll start a pot of coffee."

Chapter Nine

Christmas morning was joyful chaos, the younger kids tearing into their packages and squealing with delight at the contents. Juliana watched them with a smile, as did Lincoln and Tom, Wes and Kate. Ben and Rose-of-Sharon had joined them for breakfast with the baby, and so had the other ranch hands.

Theresa opened her gifts slowly, while Joseph examined the first one—a set of watercolors Lincoln had given him—leaving the others unwrapped beside him on the floor.

Juliana, quietly happy, paused often to admire the gold

wedding band Lincoln had given her late the night before in their bedroom. They'd made love afterward—Lincoln had taken his time pleasuring her, and the wonder of it still reverberated through her, when she let herself remember, like the aftershocks of an earthquake.

There had been no pain, only a little soreness afterward. Juliana had been as voracious as Lincoln, reveling in eager surrender, but that hadn't been the best part, nor had the ring.

When they'd gone to their room, after several hours spent visiting with Wes and his shy but delightful Kate around the kitchen table, Lincoln had sat her down on the edge of the bed, knelt before her and taken her hands into his.

He'd looked directly into her eyes, cleared his throat out of a nervousness she would always remember with tenderness, and said, "Juliana, I love you."

And she'd replied in kind. If she hadn't already loved him, that declaration, and the way he made it, would have sealed the matter for sure.

They were midway through dinner, Tom having roasted the two turkeys to perfection, when the inevitable happened.

A buggy appeared in the side yard beyond the kitchen windows, and Mr. Philbert drew back hard on the reins.

Juliana barely stifled a gasp.

Laughing at a raucous story Wes had just told, no one else had seen or heard the buggy's approach.

Lincoln, catching sight of the look on Juliana's face, turned in his chair and saw the small man alighting, righteous indignation apparent in his every move. "Is that him?" he asked.

Juliana nodded, afraid she'd burst into tears if she spoke.

Mr. Philbert had reached the back step. He pounded on the door, his fist still raised when Lincoln swung it open.

Everyone fell silent, and Daisy and Billy-Moses both rushed to Juliana and scrambled onto her lap, clinging to her.

The Indian agent wore an avidly righteous expression as he stepped past Lincoln, all his attention fastened on Juliana. Triumph sparked in his tiny eyes, behind the smudged lenses of his spectacles; he'd planned to arrive early all along, just as she'd feared, hoping to take her unawares, circumvent any steps she might take to avoid him. She *had* hoped to have Joseph and Theresa safely away from Stillwater Springs before he got there, but that was not to be.

Tom and Wes both slid back their chairs to stand.

Kate, sitting next to Theresa, slipped a protective arm around the girl's shoulders.

Philbert ignored them all, his gaze riveted on Juliana, trying to make her wilt. Jabbing an ink-stained index finger in her direction, he finally spoke. "I have half a mind to charge you with kidnapping!"

"Watch what you say to my wife," Lincoln said evenly.

Wes stepped in, exuding charm and hospitality. "Sit down," he told Mr. Philbert. "Have some of our Christmas dinner."

A silence fell. Clearly, Mr. Philbert had not expected the invitation.

Wes found a clean plate and silverware. Gave up his own chair so the unwanted guest would have a place to sit.

Looking baffled and taking in the spread of food with undisguised hunger, Mr. Philbert sat down.

Lincoln, after exchanging glances with Wes, returned to his own chair. Reached for Juliana's hand and squeezed it reassuringly.

Tom took Mr. Philbert's plate and filled it to overflowing with turkey, mashed potatoes, green beans and rolls still warm from the oven in the cookstove.

Mr. Philbert hesitated, and then, to Juliana's amazement, began to eat.

"My wife and I intend to adopt Daisy and Bill," Lincoln said after a few moments. "I've drawn up the papers, and I'll see that they're filed right after Christmas."

Both Daisy and Billy-Moses looked at Lincoln curiously, not understanding, but probably instinctively hopeful. Both of them adored Lincoln; he had a way of including them in the expansive warmth of his attention and affection without excluding Gracie.

Juliana held the little ones tightly in both arms.

His mouth full of mashed potatoes, Mr. Philbert couldn't answer.

Joseph spoke up. "I'm taking my sister home," he said. "And if you try to stop us, we'll just run off the first chance we get."

Mr. Philbert chewed, swallowed. He was red in the jowls, and his muttonchop whiskers bobbed. He waved a dismissive hand at Joseph. "Good riddance," he said. "I've got all the problems I need as it is."

Juliana's heart rose on a swell of relief, even though his attitude stung. Was that all *any* of the children whose lives and educations he oversaw were to him? Problems? Daisy and Billy-Moses huddled closer, and Gracie came to stand at her side, staring at Mr. Philbert.

"You have a big nose," the child remarked charitably.

"Gracie," Juliana said. "That will be enough."

"Well, he does. And it's purple on the end."

"Gracie," Lincoln admonished.

Gracie subsided, leaning against Juliana now. She hadn't been deliberately rude; there was no meanness in her. She'd merely been making an observation.

Juliana shifted so she could wrap one arm around the little girl without sending Daisy toppling to the floor.

"Children," Mr. Philbert said with a long-suffering sigh. "They are such troublesome little creatures."

Juliana longed to refute that statement—there were a thousand things she wanted to say, but she held her tongue. It would not do to give the man a reason to dislike her even more than he already did.

"Nevertheless," he went on, taking clear and unflattering satisfaction in his power over all of them, "duty is duty. Adoption or none, I intend to take the little ones back to Missoula with me for the interim. I have to account for them, you know."

Tom's face turned hard, and he started to rise.

Wes, standing just behind him and to the side, having given up his chair to Mr. Philbert, laid a warning hand on Tom's shoulder.

"Now, why would you want to go to all the trouble to drag them all the way to Missoula?" Lincoln asked, with a sort of easy bewilderment. "They're fine right here, part of a family."

Mr. Philbert reddened again, stabbed his fork into a slice of turkey. "According to the storekeeper in town, you and Mr. Creed are married now. Is that true, Juliana?"

He'd spoken to Mr. Willand, Juliana concluded disconsolately. That was how he'd known about the marriage—the reverend had probably scattered the news far and wide—and where to find her and the children.

"It's true," Juliana said.

"Awfully convenient," Mr. Philbert remarked, with an unpleasant smile. "Wouldn't you agree?"

Gracie took issue. "Don't you talk to my mama in that tone of voice," she warned.

That time, neither Lincoln nor Juliana scolded her.

Mr. Philbert raised his eyebrows, took the time to fork in, chew and swallow more turkey before responding. The law was on his side, as far as Juliana knew. He had the upper hand, and he wasn't going to let anyone forget that.

Daisy, uncomprehending and frightened nonetheless, turned her face into Juliana's bodice and began to cry silently, her small shoulders trembling. Juliana kissed the top of her head, stroked her raven-black hair.

"I don't think I've ever seen an Indian cry before," Mr. Philbert mused, sparing no notice for the child's obvious grief and fear.

Tom started to his feet again; Wes stopped him by putting that same hand to his shoulder and pressing him back down.

"Daisy," Lincoln said to Mr. Philbert, his voice measured, the voice of a lawyer in court, "is a *child*. She's three years old. You're scaring her, and that's something that I won't tolerate for any reason."

"I have legal authority—"

"So do I," Lincoln broke in evenly. "This is my house. This is my ranch. And if you want to take these children anywhere, you're going to need a court order and half the United States Army to help you. *Do* you have a court order, Mr. Philbert?"

Mr. Philbert sputtered a little. "Well, no, but—"

"You'd better get one, then. Before you manage that,

I'll have been to Helena to file the petition and Daisy and Bill will be Creeds, as much my children in the eyes of the law as Gracie here."

Mr. Philbert considered that, gulped, then worked up a faltering smile and asked, "I don't suppose there's any pie?"

An hour later, having topped off his meal with two slices of mincemeat pie, the agent handed Juliana a bank draft covering her last month's salary, warned her that if she should ever apply for any teaching position, anywhere, she should not give his name as a reference.

And then, blessedly, he was gone.

TAKING NO CHANCES, LEST Mr. Philbert had a change of heart, Tom and Lincoln were up even earlier than usual the next morning. They hitched up the team and wagon while Juliana helped Joseph and Theresa pack for their journey. Once the two young people were on board a train east, with Tom to escort them, Lincoln would travel to Helena, stand before a judge and enter the petition to adopt Daisy and Billy-Moses.

Juliana was afraid to hope the Bureau of Indian Affairs would not step in. At the same time, something within her sang a silent, swelling song of jubilation.

Although she tried to keep up a good front, Juliana despaired as she watched Joseph and Theresa buttoning up the new coats Lincoln had given them for Christmas. They would miss her and the other children, she knew, but the joy of going home, of truly belonging somewhere, shone in their faces.

Juliana hugged both of them, one and then the other, but avoided looking through the window after they'd gone out, unable to watch as they got into the wagon. There would be letters, at least from Theresa, but considering the distance, it was unlikely that she would ever see them again. Eventually, their correspondence would slow, however good everyone's intentions were, and finally stop.

Gracie, standing at Juliana's side, took her hand. "Don't be sad, Mama," she said. "Please, don't be sad."

But Juliana couldn't help crying as she took Gracie into her arms.

Lincoln returned to the house to say goodbye. "I'll be back in a few days," he said. "Ben and the others will look after the cattle and the chores. If Philbert comes back here, send somebody to town to fetch Wes."

Juliana nodded, barely able to absorb any of it. The

parting from Lincoln was, in some ways, the hardest thing of all.

He gave her a lingering kiss.

Then he, too, was gone.

Billy-Moses, who had sat quietly near the stove during all the farewells, stacking blocks, knocking them down and then stacking them again, suddenly hurtled toward the door, flinging himself at it, struggling with the latch and uttering long cries of angry sorrow. Juliana hurried to the child, knelt beside him, pulling him into her arms, stroking his hair, murmuring to him.

He wailed for Theresa, for Joseph, for Lincoln, sobbing out each name in turn, between shrieks of despair. Weeping herself, while Gracie and Daisy looked on with forlorn expressions, each clasping the other's hand, Juliana lifted Billy-Moses up and carried him to the rocking chair.

He was a long time quieting down, but Juliana rocked him, holding him tightly long after he'd stopped struggling. Eventually, he fell into a fitful sleep.

Gracie came to lean against the arm of the chair, her face earnest. "Doesn't Billy want to be my brother? Doesn't he want to be a Creed?"

Juliana, more composed by then, smiled and tilted her

head so it rested against Gracie's. "Of course he does, sweetheart," she said very quietly. "He misses Joseph and Theresa, that's all. And your papa and Tom, too."

Gracie nodded solemnly, but quickly braced up. "Papa said he'd come back, and Papa always does what he says he's going to do."

"Yes," Juliana agreed, heartened. "He does."

The next day, Wes returned to the ranch, bringing a telegram from Lincoln, sent that morning from Missoula. Tom, Theresa and Joseph had boarded the train; they would be in North Dakota within the week.

To keep busy, Juliana divided her time between giving Gracie reading, spelling and arithmetic lessons at the kitchen table, visiting Rose-of-Sharon and the baby, and poring over a collection of old cookery books she'd found in a pantry cabinet.

Lincoln sent another telegram the following day when he reached Helena, promising that he'd be home soon.

Determined to use the waiting time constructively, Juliana bravely assembled the ingredients to bake a batch of corn bread, followed the directions to the letter, and almost set the kitchen on fire by putting too much wood in the stove.

On the third day, the previously mild weather turned nasty. Snow flew with such ferocity that, often, Juliana couldn't see the barn from the kitchen window, even in broad daylight. She knew that Lincoln planned to return to Missoula from Helena by rail, once he'd completed his business in the state capital, reclaim his wagon and team from a local livery stable and drive back to the ranch. With what appeared to be a blizzard brewing, Juliana was worried.

He could get lost in the storm, even freeze to death somewhere along the way.

In an effort to distract herself from this worry, Juliana carefully removed all the decorations from the Christmas tree, packing them away in their boxes. When Ben Gainer brought a bucket of milk to the back door that evening, shivering with cold even in his warm coat, Juliana made him come inside and drink hot coffee.

Somewhat restored after that, Ben dragged the big tree across the floor and out the front door. Later, it would be chopped up and burned.

The storm continued through the night, and snow was still coming down at a furious rate in the morning, drifting up against the sides of the house, high enough that if she'd been able to open a window, Juliana could have scooped the stuff up in her hands.

Ben brought more milk, and told Juliana he hoped the snow would let up soon, because he and the other two ranch hands were having a hard time getting the hay sled out to the range cattle, even with the big draft horses to pull it.

One question thudded in the back of Juliana's mind day and night like a drumbeat that never went silent.

Where was Lincoln?

She tried to be sensible. He'd probably had to stay in Missoula to wait out the storm, and sent another telegram informing her of that. Since the road between Stillwater Springs and the ranch was under at least three feet of snow, Wes wouldn't be able to bring her the message, like he had the others.

There was nothing to do but wait.

Juliana tried the corn bread recipe again, and even though it came out hard as a horseshoe, at least this time smoke didn't pour out of the oven. Soaked in warm milk, the stuff was actually edible.

The next day, Ben strung ropes from the house to the cabin and the cabin to the barn; it was the only way he could get from one place to the other without being lost in the blizzard. The draft horses knew the way to and from the cluster of trees where the herd had taken shelter; otherwise, the cattle would have gone hungry.

On the fifth night, Juliana lingered in the kitchen, long after the children had gone to sleep, watching the clock and waiting.

At first, she thought she'd imagined the sound at the back door, but then the latch jiggled. She fairly leaped out of her chair, hurried across the room and hauled open the door.

The icy wind was so strong that it made her bones ache, but she didn't care. Lincoln was standing on the back step, coated in ice and snow, seemingly unable to move.

Juliana cried out, used all her strength to pull him inside and managed to shut the door against the wind by leaning on it with the full weight of her body.

"Lincoln?"

He didn't speak, didn't move. How had he gotten home with the roads the way they were? Surely the team and wagon couldn't have passed through snow that deep—it would have reached to the tops of the wheels.

She had to pry his hat free of his head—it had frozen to his hair. Next, she peeled off the coat, tossed it aside.

She thought of tugging him nearer the stove, but she recalled reading about frostbite somewhere; it was important that he warm up slowly.

His clothes were stiff as laundry left to freeze on a clothesline. She ran for the bedrooms, snatching up all the blankets she could find that weren't already in use and hurried back to the kitchen.

Lincoln was still standing where she'd left him; his lips were blue, and his teeth had begun to chatter.

"Whiskey," he said in a raw whisper.

Juliana rushed into the pantry, found the bottle he kept on a high shelf. Pouring some into a cup, she raised it to his mouth, holding it patiently while he sipped.

A great shudder went through him, but he wasn't so stiff now, and some of the color returned to his face.

"Help me out of these clothes," he ground out. "My fingers aren't working."

She pulled off his gloves first, and was relieved to see no sign of frostbite. His toes could be affected, though, and even if they weren't, the specter of pneumonia loomed in that kitchen like a third presence.

She unbuttoned his shirt, helped him out of it, then pulled his woolen undershirt off over his head, too. She immediately wrapped him in one of the blankets. He managed to sit down in the chair she brought from the table, and she crouched to pull off his boots, strip away his socks.

His toes, like his fingers, were still intact, though he admitted he couldn't feel them.

He seemed so exhausted just from what they'd done so far that Juliana gave him another dose of whiskey before removing his trousers and tucking more blankets in around him.

"How did you get here?" she asked as he sat there shivering, a good distance from the stove. "My Lord, Lincoln, you must have been out in the weather for hours."

Remarkably, a grin tilted up one corner of his mouth. "I rode Wes's mule out from town," he answered slowly, groping for each word. "Good thing that critter can smell hay and a warm stall from a mile off."

"You rode Wes's mule?" If Juliana hadn't been so glad he was home, she would have been furious. "Lincoln Creed, are you insane? If you got as far as Stillwater Springs—and God knows how you managed that—you should have stayed there!"

"You're here," he said. "Gracie and Bill and Daisy are here. This is where I belong."

"You could have frozen to death! What good would that have done us?"

He didn't respond to that question. Instead, he said, "You'd better get some snow to pack around my feet and hands, or else I might lose a few fingers and toes."

The action was contrary to every instinct Juliana possessed, but she knew he was right. After bundling up, she took the milk bucket outside and filled it with snow.

Returning to the kitchen, she marveled that Lincoln had been able to travel in that weather, probably for hours, when she'd been chilled to her marrow by a few moments in the backyard.

The process of tending to Lincoln was slow and, for him, painful. It was after two in the morning when he told her there had been enough of the snow packs. She led him to their room, put him to bed like a child, piling blanket after blanket on top of him.

Still he shivered.

She built the hearth fire up until it roared.

Lying in the darkness, under all those blankets, he chuckled. "Juliana, no more wood," he said. "You'll set the house on fire."

There was nothing more she could do except put on

her nightgown and join him. He trembled so hard that the whole bed frame shook, and his skin felt as cold as stone.

She huddled close to him, sharing the warmth of her own body, enduring the chill of his. When he finally slept, she could not, exhausted as she was, because she was so afraid of waking up to find him dead.

For most of the night, she kept her vigil. Then, too tired to keep her eyes open for another moment, she drifted off.

When she woke up, his hand was underneath her nightgown.

"There's one way you could warm me up," he said wickedly.

He was safe.

He was warm again, and well.

And Juliana gladly gave herself up to him.

Epilogue

June 1911

Juliana Creed stood in Willand's Mercantile, visibly pregnant and beaming as she read Theresa's most recent letter through for the second time before folding it carefully and tucking it into her handbag. She and Joseph had attended a small school on the reservation since their return to North Dakota, but now they would have the whole summer off. Joseph had a temporary job milking cows on a nearby farm, while Theresa would be helping her grandmother tend the garden.

Juliana looked around the store for her children.

Billy-Moses—now called just Bill or Billy most of the time, a precedent Lincoln had set—was examining a toy train carved out of wood, while Daisy and Gracie browsed through hair ribbons, ready-made dresses with ruffles, and storybooks.

With all of them accounted for, her mind turned to the men. Tom was at the blacksmith's, having a horse shod, and Lincoln had gone to the *Courier,* looking for Wes.

Marriage had changed Weston Creed. He was, as Lincoln put it, "damn near to becoming a respectable citizen." Remarkably, given the long estrangement between her and Wes, the elder Mrs. Creed had returned to Stillwater Springs for the wedding back in April. While she hadn't been happy about having a saloonkeeper for a daughter-in-law, she'd behaved with remarkable civility.

Cora had stayed long enough to size Juliana up, decided she'd do as a wife for Lincoln and a stepmother for Gracie, and then she'd announced that she was taking up permanent residence with her cousins in Phoenix. She was too old, she maintained, to keep going back and forth.

Although they'd been a little stiff with each other at first, Juliana had soon come to like her mother-in-law.

While Cora had been cool to Kate, she *had* made the long journey home to attend the wedding. During her stay at the ranch, she'd treated Daisy and Billy as well as she had Gracie.

Before her departure, though, Cora and Juliana had agreed, in a spirit of goodwill, that one Creed woman per household was plenty.

When the little bell over the mercantile chimed, Juliana turned in the direction of the door, expecting to see Lincoln, or perhaps Tom.

Her heart missed a beat when she recognized Clay.

Their eyes met, but neither of them spoke.

Clay stood just over the threshold, handsome in his well-tailored suit. His hair was darker than Juliana's, more chestnut than red, but his eyes were the same shade of blue.

Watching her, he removed his very fashionable hat. "Juliana," he said gravely, with a slight nod.

"Clay," Juliana whispered. And then she ran to him, threw her arms around him.

Tentatively, he put his arms around her, too. After a stiff moment, he hugged her back. "You're looking well," he said, his voice gruff with emotion.

Juliana blushed, confounded by joy, pushing back far

enough to look up into her brother's face. "When you didn't answer my letter, I thought—"

He smiled, glancing down at her protruding middle. "You did say you were married?" he teased.

She showed him her wedding ring. "How long have you been in town? The train came through three days ago."

"I've been staying at the Comstock Hotel, trying to work up the courage to hire a buggy over at the livery stable and drive out to the ranch to see you."

"Oh, Clay—surely you knew you'd be welcome."

"I *didn't* know," he replied. "According to my wife, I've been behaving like an ogre ever since you refused to marry John Holden, and I'm afraid Nora's right about that."

Juliana's eyes misted over. "I've missed you," she said.

He kissed her forehead. "I'd like to meet this husband of yours," he told her. "Your letter made him sound like a paragon."

The door opened again, and Lincoln was there.

Still tearful—tears came more easily with her pregnancy—Juliana moved to Lincoln's side. He put an arm around her, regarding Clay curiously and then with a grin of recognition.

"You must be Clay Mitchell," he said. "With eyes that color, you have to be related to Juliana."

Clay nodded in acknowledgment. "And you're Lincoln Creed," he replied.

"Papa!" Billy yelled, racing across the store to be hoisted into Lincoln's arms. Lincoln ruffled the boy's hair and laughed.

Clay's eyes widened momentarily, but then he smiled again.

"Daisy," Juliana called, "Gracie—come and meet your uncle Clay."

He charmed those two little girls by executing a gentlemanly bow. "Ladies," he said solemnly, making them giggle.

Still carrying Billy, Lincoln excused himself and went to the counter to speak to Fred Willand about their grocery order.

"You will come out to the ranch and stay with us for a few days, won't you, Clay?" Juliana asked quietly.

"I'd be glad to," Clay assured her.

On the way home, having collected his bag from the hotel, Clay rode on the wagon seat next to Juliana with Lincoln at the reins, while Gracie, Billy and Daisy bounced along in back like always, seated among crates of groceries.

"He doesn't seem so bad to me," Lincoln said much later, when he and Juliana had retired to their room for the night. They'd talked right through supper, the three of them, and for a couple of hours afterward.

"This is the Clay I knew before," Juliana said, choking up a little. The change in her brother seemed miraculous.

Sitting on the edge of the bed, Lincoln pulled off one boot and then the other. Juliana remembered the night he'd ridden a mule through three feet of snow, nearly losing his fingers and toes, if not his life.

"I've never had a sister," Lincoln said, "but I can imagine that if I did, I might have some pretty hard-headed opinions about what she should and shouldn't do."

Juliana stood in front of the mirror, brushing her hair. "We were so young when our mother died," she mused. She'd long since told Lincoln all about her family history, John Holden and his daughters, secretly studying to be a teacher when her grandmother believed she was in finishing school. "Clay's a little older, and I guess I expected him to be strong, maybe our grandmother did, too. But he was really a child, as scared and lost and hurt as I was. I hate to think what must have gone through his mind when our father left us at Grandmama's that day. Clay knew, even if I didn't, that Father wasn't coming back—and that meant he had to be a man from then on."

Lincoln came to stand behind her, bent his head to kiss her right ear. His hands caressed her round belly. "That corn bread you served at supper tonight was pretty good," he said.

She laughed. "It should have been," she replied. "I've been practicing for six months."

He took the brush from her hand, set it aside on the bureau, turned her around to face him. "Tom says you'll make a fine cook one of these days."

Juliana smiled. Tom had been giving her cookery lessons, and she was making progress. "He also says I try too hard." She slipped her arms around his middle and leaned against him. "What else can I do? I want to keep my husband happy."

Lincoln tasted her mouth, once, twice, a third time. "Your husband," he said, "is *very* happy."

She looked up at him. "I love you, Lincoln Creed. Just when I think I couldn't possibly love you more than I already do, something happens to prove me wrong."

"I love you, too," he replied, tracing the length of her cheek, and then her neck, with the lightest pass of his lips. He eased her toward the bed, still nibbling at her.

He put out the lamp.

"Lincoln, you're not listening to me," Juliana said, laughing a little, as delightfully nervous, in some ways, as she'd been on their wedding night.

He lowered her to the bed. "You're right," he said, kissing her again. "I'm not."

Already cherishing their unborn child, Lincoln was unspeakably tender as he caressed her belly and then slowly raised her nightgown, first to her knees, then her thighs, then her shoulders. With a groan of welcome, she raised her arms so he could slip the garment off over her head.

He kissed her distended stomach, his lips warm and faintly moist.

Juliana groaned again, rolled her eyes back in contentment and closed them, giving herself up to Lincoln, body, mind and spirit.

He loved the fullness of her breasts, kissed and nibbled at her taut nipples until she said his name in a ragged whisper.

Then he moved down along her breastbone, over her middle, pausing at her abdomen before using his fingers to part the nest of curls at the juncture of her thighs. She whimpered as he stroked her with a slow, gentle motion of his hand, and although her eyes remained shut, she felt the dark burn of his gaze on her face. She knew he was silently asking her permission, and she nodded.

He made a sound that was wholly male, low in his throat.

In Lincoln's arms, Juliana had learned a sort of pleasure that she'd never imagined, and that night was no exception. Even before they'd conceived this child they both wanted so much, he'd always been careful, raising her to an explosive ecstasy and at the same time making her feel utterly safe.

For a time, he simply made slow circles with his fingers, and Juliana began to writhe in need and surrender, in triumph and exultation.

Her breath became shallow and rapid as he teased her. Then the first release came, shattering and sweet, leaving her shuddering. Knowing there would be more—much more—before the night was over, only increased her wanting.

Lincoln used his mouth on her next, and though it was scandalous, Juliana gloried in the intimacy of it, in the helplessness and the sheer power of the sensations he wrought in her, with every nibble, every flick of his tongue.

Again, she broke apart in a million fiery pieces, a

primitive cry of satisfaction escaping her throat, but going no further than the thick log walls of their bedroom.

Only when Lincoln was certain he'd untied every knot in Juliana's still-quivering body did he mount her, and ease into her depths with that heartrending tenderness she'd come to expect of him.

They rocked together, and she reached yet another pinnacle, softer and yet more intense than the others that had gone before. When Lincoln finally let himself go, Juliana finally opened her eyes, stroking his strong shoulders, his chest, his sides, her hands moving in ways that both soothed and inflamed.

Then he tensed upon her, and she felt life itself spill within her, the life that had brought their child into being, and Gracie, as well.

"I love you," Juliana whispered.

He sighed, kissed her cheek, her neck. Fell beside her. "And I love *you*, Juliana Creed."

IF JULIANA HAD YET TO MASTER cooking and housekeeping, she *had* learned to drive a buggy. On the morning of Clay's departure for Denver, she was the one who drove him to the depot in town.

"I've got eyes," Clay said, grinning, as they pulled up to await the train, "but I still need to hear you say it. Are you happy, Juliana?"

She kissed his cheek. "Ecstatic," she said, meaning it.

He reached into the inside pocket of his coat—his fine clothes made him stand out like the proverbial sore thumb in rustic Stillwater Springs—and brought out a thick envelope. Offered it to her.

In the distance, the train whistle shrilled.

Puzzled, Juliana looked at the envelope, then at Clay's face. "What…?"

"Your inheritance," Clay said. "These documents transfer full control to you. You're a rich woman, Juliana. Now that I've taken Lincoln Creed's measure, I know you'll be all right."

Stunned—it had been a long time since she'd given a thought to money—she accepted the papers. Then she beamed. "Now we can build a hay barn right on the range," she chimed in happy realization. "And the cattle will have somewhere to take shelter when the snows come."

Clay laughed. "Some women would want diamonds, or fine dresses."

The train chugged into view, and Juliana saddened a

little at the sight, not willing to be parted from this brother she had loved for so long. "You'll come back when you can, won't you? And bring Nora and the children?"

He touched her cheek. "We'll be here," he said. "And you're welcome at our place anytime, Juliana. You and Lincoln and this brood of yours."

With that, he climbed down from the buggy, took his traveling case from under the seat. He looked up at her, winked, and then turned away, walking purposefully toward the depot.

Juliana waited until the train had pulled out before heading for home.

Lincoln was there, having minded the children while she was gone, and Ben and Rose-of-Sharon sat at the table, baby Joshua in his mother's arms. For all the difficulties of his birth, the infant was thriving.

Once the Gainers had left, Juliana took the envelope from her handbag and laid it on the table.

"What's this?" Lincoln asked.

"Open it," Juliana said lightly, "and read for yourself."

Lincoln hesitated, then did as he was told. His eyes widened as he read. "That's one hell of a lot of money," he said finally. "You are a wealthy woman, Juliana."

"*We* are wealthy," she clarified.

He grinned, and only then did she realize how tensely he'd held his shoulders while he read. Had he thought, for the briefest moment, that she'd leave him now that she was a woman of independent means?

She went to him, slipped her arms around his lean, hard waist. "I told Clay we'd be building a big hay barn out on the range, first thing."

Lincoln chuckled. "Speaking of the range, I'd better get out there. We've still got a few calves taking their time to get born."

Juliana began rolling up her sleeves. "I'll have supper ready when you get back," she said.

He gave a comical wince, and she slapped at him playfully.

Once he'd gone, Juliana took a deep breath. It was time to make another attempt at corn bread.

From the *Stillwater Springs Courier*:

September 18, 1911
This editor is proud to announce the
birth of a nephew,
Michael Thomas Creed.
Welcome.